Haunted Journey

a novel by Wendy B. Truscott

Loon Echo Publications

www.wendytruscott.com | www.facebook.com/hauntedjourney

ISBN
978-0-9952108-2-0 (ebook)
978-0-9952108-1-3 (ebook)
Also issued in paperback format 978-0-9952108-0-6

Cover: Steven Novak www.novakillustration.com
Editor: Caroline Kaiser www.carolinekaiser.com

Outline map of Ontario (altered) : Brock University Map, Data &
GIS Library. Available: Brock University Map, Data & GIS Library
Controlled Access https://brocku.ca/maplibrary/maps/outline/
(Accessed April 27, 2010).

Partial Map of Muskoka (not to scale): Wendy Truscott
Lyrics Wind Beneath My Wings: Bette Middler

1.Muskoka, Family Relationships, Loss of Parent, Teens, Middle Grade,
History, Settlers, Pioneers, Lake of Bays, Baysville, Bracebridge, Gravenhurst.

Dedication

For my children-Heather, Shelley, and Paul, Jr.,

the sunshine in my life.

My grandchildren- Samantha, Briar, Chantal, and Caleb,

the jewels in my crown,

my daughter-in-law, Tara, and son-in-law, Peter, the blessed additions to

our family,

and for Paul, who promised to love, honour, and cherish, and who has,

"You are the wind beneath my wings."

TABLE OF CONTENTS

Chapter 1 Caleb

Chapter 2 Caleb's Dilemma

Chapter 3 Samantha

Chapter 4 The Day Everything Changed

Chapter 5 Three Sisters

Chapter 6 Rabbit Stew and Visitors Too

Chapter 7 Two Fierce Mothers

Chapter 8 Danger in the Woods

Chapter 9 A Strange Turn of Events

Chapter 10 Almost Home

Chapter 11 Andrew

Chapter 12 A Day of Surprises

Chapter 13 A Close Call

Chapter 14 Family Reunion

Chapter 15 Reality Sets In

Chapter 16 Catching Up

Chapter 17 Bedtime Stories

Chapter 18 Big Shoes to Fill

Chapter 19 Samantha's Dilemma

Chapter 20 The Stranger Returns

Chapter 21 A Turn for the Better

Chapter 22 Good News

Chapter 23 Thief

Chapter 24 A Letter from Afar

Chapter 25 Andrew's Nightmare

Chapter 26 Meeting Miss Heather

Chapter 27 Eavesdropping

Chapter 28 Keeping Secrets

Chapter 29 Back to School

Chapter 30 Samantha's Question

Chapter 31 Caleb's Story

Chapter 32 Preparing for a Social Call

Chapter 33 Tea and Scones for the Teacher

Chapter 34 Conversations

Chapter 35 Catching Dreams

Chapter 36 An Offering of Hope

Chapter 37 Caleb and Andrew

Chapter 38 Threatening Rumours

Chapter 39 Confrontation

Chapter 40 A Family Meeting

Chapter 41 A Visit to the Doctor

Chapter 42 Storm

Chapter 43 Rough Water

Chapter 44 Caleb's Challenge

Chapter 45 Storm's Aftermath

Chapter 46 Saying Goodbye

Chapter 47 Haunted House

Chapter 48 The Party

Chapter 49 Christmas Eve

"A journey of a thousand miles begins with a single step."

-Lao Tzu

"The only journey is the one within."

-Rainier Maria Riilke

Map of Ontario Showing Muskoka District

Partial Map of Muskoka Showing Locations in Haunted Journey

CHAPTER ONE

Caleb

Caleb Lawson had never been so tired in his life. He stumbled along the dusty road like a sleepwalker, unaware of his surroundings. When the quiet of the nearby woods erupted into a violent crashing and thrashing, his half-closed eyes flew open. *What the . . . ?* Dazed and startled, he tripped, flying forward. Fighting to stay upright, he felt his right knee twist, and an intense pain jolted him fully awake. A loud gasp escaped his lips before he could suck in his breath and listen.

Bear? Moose? Wolf? Caleb's mind raced through the possibilities. With only a small knife to defend himself, his options were limited. *Damn! I could use a shotgun right now! All I can do is try to run.* He knew he couldn't expect to get far now that he'd hurt his knee.

Several heart-stopping minutes passed with no further loud noises before he allowed his body to relax. *Most likely just a dead old tree crashing to the ground. Sure hope so!* He didn't think he could cope with any large wild animals. *Got to stay alert!* he reminded himself.

To add to the burden of his total exhaustion, he felt as if his throbbing knee might be sprained. Rolling up his pant leg revealed a large bruise and the beginning of a swelling lump. *Blast it!* Looking around, he noticed what must have tripped him: the tip of a log heaved up from the road. Caleb was so furious, he could have kicked it. "That would really help!" he muttered to himself, rubbing his knee. *Blast the log, and blast this damn road!* He wiped his sweating brow.

Without the protection of the battered straw hat he'd lost days ago, his fair hair had become filthy and as dry as straw, and his normally pale skin stung from the brilliant red sunburn on his dust-coated neck and face. The burn was the result of falling into a deep sleep in full sun on the same day he lost his hat. He'd only meant to sit down and rest for a few minutes, but heat and fatigue had overpowered him.

Today's path was wide enough to allow some sun in, so he had been trying to keep to the shady side. He thought of stopping and resting soon but was unwilling to do so, just in case that noise hadn't been a tree falling but something more menacing. Massaging his knee a little and trying to ignore the pain, he willed himself forward.

It was going to be slow going, Caleb realized after several hobbling steps. He paused and took a deep breath. As he did so, a cool, prickly sensation crept up the back of his neck like icy fingers; he had the feeling of being watched. Whipping around, he almost lost his balance because of his protesting knee and was so shaken by what he was seeing that he felt as if his heart had dropped into his stomach. On the path, not fifty feet away from him, stood an enormous, long-legged creature, the tallest he'd ever seen. A moose bearing an enormous rack of antlers stared him down.

That must be what made all that noise in the bush, he realized. *And I thought it was a falling tree! Wow! Those antlers have to be at least five feet wide!* He'd heard stories of the damage a moose could do, and here he stood, alone and defenceless. Once again he wished he had a gun. He considered shouting and waving his arms at the giant in hopes of scaring it off but decided that might have the opposite effect; instead he might anger it, and he sure didn't want to do that!

The moose stretched its neck, its flared nostrils smelling the air for danger. Piercing wide brown eyes seemed to be sizing Caleb up. Blackflies buzzed around those eyes, and the mighty head shook in annoyance. *So that's what brought him out of the woods. He's trying to get away from the flies.*

Caleb stood rooted to the ground, trying to decide what to do. All the while he kept his eyes on the moose. Should he remain still or try moving away very slowly? If he tried to get away, would the towering creature come after him?

Moose only eat leaves and plants, he reminded himself. *Still, those antlers could toss me a long way into the bush and those hooves . . .* Trembling, he chanced a step backwards.

The moose continued to stare directly at him; then, after shaking its head and those gigantic antlers in a slow side-to-side arc, it moved one long leg forward. Caleb stood as rigid as a tent pole, afraid to breathe. That leg was almost as tall as he was! When the moose took another lumbering step, its body began a slow turn and Caleb realized it wasn't coming for him; it was moving back into the woods! Still, he didn't move until he was certain.

Only after the animal's hindquarters had disappeared into the trees did he let out his breath and dare to turn his back. Taking up his journey again, he continued looking over his shoulder every few steps until he'd convinced himself the moose was long gone. Growing up in the woods, he'd often seen moose before but never one so huge, and never when he'd felt so vulnerable and alone.

Another two miles or so farther on, a copse of young birches at the edge of a quiet field offered an inviting spot to rest. Caleb decided he had probably put enough distance between himself and the moose, so giving in to his pain and fatigue at last, he limped off the road, lay down out of the sun's reach, and spread out his tired and grateful body. He tried not to think about any other wild animals that might be hidden nearby.

Sweet-smelling grass and the chirping of heat bugs lulled him, and even though an annoying fly buzzed near his head, within seconds he was dreaming—not pleasant dreams of happy times, but terrifying ones of his little sisters screaming in the dark, crying because their bellies were empty and calling his name.

"Caleb! Where are you? Come home! We need you. Please, Caleb. Please come home!"

Tossing around on the lumpy ground, he tried to find a flatter and softer spot. The horrendous dreams were not new; they had terrorized him for several weeks now and were the reason for his journey. The nightmares haunted him, refused him rest, and propelled him home. *What does it all mean?* he wondered. *I have to find out.*

CHAPTER TWO

Caleb's Dilemma

Stretched out in the shaded patch of long grass by the side of the road, Caleb felt for the old sock sewn inside the waist at the back of his trousers. *Still there! Good.* With its weight evenly distributed, it appeared flat. No one would suspect what he carried. To some, it wouldn't be much, but to him, it was treasure. He hoped it would also be a peace offering of sorts.

Why did I just sneak away that morning? Makes me look like a coward. I hate that! Could have at least left a note, but heck, I was only thirteen! Couldn't think how else to do it.

Now he wondered what to expect when they all saw him. After all, it had been more than two years. Would his parents be angry? Would his mother cry? *Sure hope not. I couldn't take it. I'd feel even more guilty. They probably all hate me!*

He hadn't been able to talk to his parents about how he was feeling because he could see they were struggling and worn out too. Besides, in the last few months before he left, his outgoing father had become more and more withdrawn and quiet, and that was scary.

His sisters would have changed in two years. *I wonder if little Chantal will even remember me.* The thought that she might think he was a stranger made him sad. He knew he'd changed too. He'd been slim to start with, but now his ribs showed, and he'd grown so tall he looked like . . . "like a string bean!" A familiar, teasing voice seemed to whisper the words in his ear, interrupting his gloomy thoughts. *Mother!* For a moment, Caleb's heart lifted as he looked around, almost expecting to see her, until he realized he was simply recalling a long-ago moment when his mother had used that expression.

He pictured his sisters as they had been when he left home: Samantha, a cheerful nine-year-old: Briar, six, quieter and shy; and Chantal, barely three, still a baby in his eyes. He knew Samantha and Briar had adored their big brother. They'd remember him for sure, and he had a feeling they'd also be relieved and glad to see him. After all, they were calling to him in those dreams.

He'd missed all of them and hoped that his parents, especially his father, wouldn't be so angry with him that they'd tell him he wasn't welcome and ask him to leave. He had no idea what he'd do if they did, so best not to think about it.

Soon all these thoughts made him anxious, and he continued to worry about what his dreams might mean. Rising with some stiffness, Caleb stepped onto the road once more. To keep his mind from dwelling on his painful knee and his encounter with the moose, he sang a marching song he remembered learning when he was little. *Why not? There's no one around to hear. Besides, it might help scare off anything else that's lurking out there!*

> "The grand old Duke of York,
> He had ten thousand men.
> He marched them up to the top of the hill,
> Then marched them down again.

And when they were up, they were up,
And when they were down, they were down.
And when they were only half-way up,
They were neither up nor down!"

Caleb laughed to himself, *That one's all right, but it's really a baby's song.* Besides, it was too short to keep repeating for very long, but he did love stories and songs about soldiers. He began to sing one of his favourites:

"O'er the hills and o'er the main,
Through Flanders, Portugal and Spain.
King George commands and we obey
Over the hills and far away."

There were several more verses, but today he was too tired to remember all of them.

He began a tuneless humming, just for the sake of making a noise and feeling less alone. Before he knew it, he was singing strange words that seemed to belong to the tune.

"John Brown's body lies a-mouldering in the grave."

Bewildered, Caleb scratched his head and wondered, *Where the heck did that come from?*

"John Brown's body lies a-mouldering in the grave,
Glory, Glory, Hallelujah . . ."

A memory surfaced of the lumber camp where he and his father had worked and the men sitting around an occasional campfire, swapping tall tales and singing. There were a couple of Yankees on the crew, and when they sang this song it became one of his father's favourites. *I wonder if Father went back this year? It was so cold and lonely,* Caleb remembered, *Hard work too! We would never have left Mother and the girls alone on the farm for so long if we hadn't needed the money so bad.* Most of their neighbours also needed the extra money they could earn logging through the winter.

Caleb finally realized there was no use trying to shut out thoughts of his family. The closer he got to home, the stronger both his memories and his nervousness became.

> "John Brown's body lies a-mouldering in the grave,
> But his soul goes marching on."

If he kept up this pace, in perhaps two days he'd be home, and then at last he'd have the answers to his questions. Why were his sisters haunting his dreams? Would his parents turn him away or welcome him home? What would the answers be?

CHAPTER THREE

Samantha

Clink! A metallic sound outside the cabin interrupted Samantha's troubled dreams. In an instant she was wide awake and listening.

What was that?

Glancing at her younger sisters, who still slept deeply, she wondered if she'd imagined it, but probably not. Creeping up to the tiny loft window above their heads, she peered down and her breath caught in her throat. She wasn't dreaming; this was a real-life nightmare! In the rosy glow of dawn, she recognized her mother's tall, lean form slowly backing away from an enormous black bear!

Samantha opened her mouth to scream, but no sound came out. In her chest, a large drum beat a wild tattoo. Clutching the windowsill, she watched the bear stop to investigate the spilled contents of an overturned bucket while Mother retreated, slowly placing each foot behind her. She moved as carefully as someone on a dangerous precipice.

Mother must have dropped the bucket when she saw the bear. The sound I heard was probably when it hit a rock, she thought.

Unable to take her eyes off the bear, Samantha didn't realize that she had been holding her breath until she heard her mother quietly open the door downstairs and enter the cabin. When she relaxed, all that pent-up breath rushed out. *Mother's safe! It's a miracle!* A quick glance out the little window again showed the bear was gone.

Scrambling over the loft floor to the ladder, she almost slid down it in her haste to be with her mother. Somehow she had managed not to awaken her sisters. *Another miracle!* Her mother leaned against the door, her eyes closed and hands over her heart, as if to stop its pounding.

"Oh, Mama! You're all right." Samantha rushed across the room, threw her arms around her surprised mother's waist, and squeezed her so tightly that her arms began to ache. When her mother hugged her just as tightly in return and kissed the top of her head, Samantha started to cry. She really wanted to be brave, but this had been too close a call.

"I saw the bear, but I didn't know what to do!"

"It's all right, darling. I'm safe." Her mother patted Samantha reassuringly on the back. "I must admit, I had quite a fright! That bear took me completely by surprise, but I'm sure I surprised it too. I hope it's gone."

"It is. I looked, and there was no sign of it."

"Well, I'm sure it's far away by now, but we'll have to keep a lookout, just in case it decides to come back. Are Briar and Chantal still asleep? I can't believe they haven't woken up," said her mother.

"They didn't hear anything."

"Well, that's all for the best, don't you think? I'm going to ask you to keep this a secret, dear. It's better if your sisters don't know."

"All right, Mama."

Her mother looked deep into her blue eyes, so much like her own, and gently stroked her hair. "You're such a good girl. I don't know what I'd do without you. I'm afraid you've had too much to deal with in the past two years, but I want you to know how proud I am of you."

Samantha couldn't reply. She was still tearful and didn't want to let go of her mother. It was less than two years since she'd lost her father and her brother, and she wasn't about to let anything happen to her mother!

"Now I'll put the kettle on!" Mother announced in a cheerful, brisk manner. "I could use a good, hot cup of tea after that bit of excitement. Would you like some breakfast now? I don't suppose you feel like going back to bed."

"I don't think I could go back to sleep, but I don't want breakfast right now either. I just want to keep hugging you," Samantha said, savouring the warmth and comfort of her mother's arms.

"I understand." Mother's voice was soft again. "I know I couldn't go back to sleep now. But I am going to have that cup of tea, and I just might take it outside so I can listen to the birds waking, like I usually do. Their morning songs will calm me."

"Outside?" Samantha couldn't believe her ears! She threw her head back and regarded her mother with amazement. "What if the bear comes back?"

"I think it's taken off for more interesting places. Besides, I'll just be sitting on the little stump right by the door, and I'll keep an eye out."

Samantha's doubts must have shown on her face. "I'll be fine, dear," her mother insisted. "The bear is gone. Try not to worry. If you do go back upstairs, go quietly. I'm not ready yet for Chantal's antics this morning!"

With reluctance, Samantha left her mother's embrace and watched her fill the kettle from the water bucket and put it on the stove. A sudden exhaustion overcame her. "I think I will go back upstairs after all," she said, yawning.

As Samantha climbed the ladder, Chantal moaned and rolled over as if she were going to wake up. Samantha stopped where she was and remained still.

Please, don't wake up! She silently pleaded with her sister. That was the last thing she needed right now. As Chantal settled, Samantha tiptoed to her own mattress beside her. She lay down on top of the blankets, her mind racing.

That bear could have killed Mother! Then we'd be orphans! What would happen to all of us? Who'd take care of us? Maybe we'd be put in an orphanage! Oh, Papa, why did you have to die? I miss you . . . and you, Caleb! Darn it, where are you? Why did you leave us? Why don't you come home?

CHAPTER FOUR

The Day Everything Changed

Samantha would never forget that April morning two years ago when Caleb had disappeared. None of the family would; it continued to haunt them all.

After realizing Caleb wasn't in the house or barn, his parents had tried to imagine some errand he might have suddenly remembered, or some other reasonable explanation for his absence.

"Did any of you hear him get up this morning? Did you hear him moving around at all, or going down the ladder? He must have made some noise!" Mother had grilled the girls, desperate for answers.

Disappointed, the girls could offer no clues.

Perhaps he'd gone into the fields early, although there was no logical reason he should have headed there before anyone else was up. Their father had saddled Bonnie and headed out to search, alerting neighbours, some of whom joined him. No one spoke of their worst fears, but it was impossible to prevent their vivid imaginations from conjuring up the most terrible visions.

The search had continued for several fruitless days before Samantha's defeated father surrendered to the inevitable conclusion. She remembered the pain of watching her parents' worn and worried expressions turn to horror when they finally realized Caleb was gone for good. She cried for days and developed severe stomach aches. Briar and Chantal were stricken and quiet, but they too cried endlessly. It was harder for them to comprehend the significance of what had happened.

The Lawson home became unbearably sad and gloomy after that. There were times when Samantha raged with bitter anger and resentment toward Caleb. How could he have left them? They were struggling and working so hard just to survive.

You should be here to help. It's not fair!

Inevitably, though, whenever she allowed herself to feel angry at her brother, feelings of guilt and shame would overwhelm her. Caleb was a good boy, and whatever had happened to him, she really couldn't imagine he'd done anything bad or gotten into serious trouble.

He was thirteen when he left, just a year and a bit older than she was now.

He'll be fifteen, almost grown. Caleb, are you still alive? If you are, why can't you let us know somehow? Samantha knew there was a possibility Caleb wasn't alive, but that was too painful to think about, so she tried hard not to.

The sound of her mother's puttering around downstairs, making her morning pot of tea, reached Samantha's ears. Then she heard her move to the shelves and, by straining her ears, could just make out the sound of coins rustling in a tin. Mother was going to count their savings again! This was a bad sign, Samantha had learned, because it indicated how worried her mother was. Every time something distressing happened, Mother poured out the contents of the tin can and counted the coins again. They didn't add up to much, but someday, if they decided they must abandon the farm, there just might be enough for train fare to Toronto.

Sometimes the family made the long walk to the general store in the village to sell or trade their hens' eggs and the socks, mitts, and scarves they knit. In this way, they were able to add a few coins to their savings.

It was hard, though, to wander around that bountiful building, jammed to the rafters with household staples and many luxuries well beyond their means. With wistful enormous eyes, the girls admired all the rolls of pretty fabric, mouth-watering penny candy, and occasionally, marvellous toys. How wonderful it would be to wear a new dress in a floral pattern, or to taste one of the striped and swirly multicoloured lollipops, or to own a real chessboard.

Maybe someday . . .

From time to time, as they sat in the early evenings knitting or mending, Mother would mention that the train now came as far north as Gravenhurst, and there were rumours it would soon be extended to Bracebridge. If they had to leave, she'd say, they would pack lightly and walk to the station. If the roads were in bad condition, or if the walk was too much for the younger girls, they could probably find a settler willing to give them shelter—likely for a price, of course. If not, they might have to camp out in a field. Mother would smile brightly at this idea, giving it an air of high adventure.

Samantha figured her mother could see her daughters' concern at this prospect—she would always add that such big decisions were a long way off.

Clearly, Mother was undecided about whether or not to leave, and Samantha didn't know what to think. Although their situation was becoming desperate, this was the only world she'd known. Father was buried here, and so were two little brothers who had lived only a few months. It would be very emotional to leave all those memories behind. Then there was Caleb. What if he returned some day, only to find they were all gone? How could they even consider leaving? Yet mother seemed convinced that without Father and Caleb, she and her girls would not be able to keep up with all the heavy work on the farm.

What would the big city be like? The thought was scary. Her grandparents were gone, and Mother's only brother had moved west to Alberta. Things would have been so much easier for all of them after Father died if Uncle Wesley had still been in Ontario. However, Mother still had a cousin in Toronto, John Hurst, who might be able to find domestic work for her. She would find a place to live, and the children could go to school regularly.

Even when she was younger, Samantha had been able read the growing despair in her father's once-jovial face. He had been so lively and so much fun, but over time his health became worse and worse. Then Caleb disappeared. It was a blow, and little more than a year later, Father died. Remembering all this brought fresh tears, which she wiped away with the hem of her nightgown. *Darn you, Caleb!*

Hearing the door creak, she realized her mother must have indeed slipped back outside to listen to the morning birds' chorus.

"Well, there are more than birds out there this morning!" Samantha wanted to say. *How could you go back out after what happened? Don't you know how scared I am?*

Frightened and confused, she realized she was also chilly and couldn't resist slipping under the cozy comforters with her sisters.

Just for a minute or two, she thought. *Because I'm cold. I won't go to sleep. I need to keep listening, in case anything more happens. Mother said she'd sit right beside the door . . .*

Samantha's abrupt early awakening, and all her worries, had exhausted her. Within moments, she fell into a deep but troubled sleep.

CHAPTER FIVE

Three Sisters

Less than an hour after she'd fallen back to sleep, Samantha was awake again. She was trying hard to pretend she was still asleep but not having much luck. Her little sister, Chantal, had been awake for most of that hour and was restless, kicking Samantha under the comforter and knocking her in the eye with her elbow as she turned and turned. Chantal, just five, was like Jack, their rooster, anxious to rise and start the day. Eight-year-old Briar whispered stories to Chantal in a futile attempt to keep her in bed a bit longer.

Finally giving in, Samantha rubbed her eyes, stretched her arms over her curly brown head, and yawned. Stretching and yawning felt luxurious, and she smiled to herself. Although it was usually very warm and stuffy in the loft, this morning a breath of cool, sweet-smelling air wafted through the small window. Then an image of the bear tracked across her mind, and she stopped smiling. She listened and was relieved to hear Mother just coming in the door.

Turning to look at her sisters, she found Briar's bright blue eyes smiling at her. They were exactly like her own. Briar's straight hair was so fair, it was almost white. Sometimes Samantha wished her hair was also straight. All those tight curls were always getting tangled, and it hurt like heck to brush them, so she usually just ran her fingers through them to restore some kind of order.

Chantal, with hazel eyes like Father's, looked solemnly at Samantha, waiting for the word that she could now start her day. She might be a real bother at times—like now when all Samantha wanted to do was sleep a bit longer—but mostly she wasn't too bad. Her light brown hair also needed a brushing after such a restless night, and Samantha gently ran her fingers through it, which Chantal loved. She was rewarded by an angelic smile on her sister's little face. Samantha was glad she hadn't woken the girls when she'd been so terrified by the sight of the bear. Mother wanted her to keep it secret. It wouldn't be easy, but she'd try.

"Time to get up?" asked Chantal. "I want to give Bonnie some carrots."

"Yes, time to get up. It's chilly, so wrap a blanket around yourself, and put your shoes on."

"My shoes hurt my feet. I growed and they hurt."

"It's about time I got new shoes," said Briar. "Mine are way too tight. Maybe if Mother can get me some new ones, you could wear mine."

"New shoes are probably too much to hope for," Samantha put in. "It's a good thing it's summer and we can go barefoot. Mine need mending, but the shoemaker hasn't made his rounds for a long time. I can almost fit into Mother's, so maybe I could wear something of hers and you can have mine. We'll just have to wait and see." Sighing, she added, "But new shoes would be wonderful!" She lay there another moment, visions of shiny new shoes making her wistful.

***

Samantha was helping Chantal down the wooden ladder from the loft when something caught her eye. She stopped and turned to look at her mother. Briar was at the top just putting her foot on the first rung and almost stepped on Chantal.

"Samantha! Keep going!"

"Move, Samantha!" cried Chantal. "I want down!"

Samantha quickly stepped off the ladder and stood staring at her mother. When the other two girls were down, they also stood transfixed. Their mother's face was wet, as if she had been crying, but on her face was the biggest smile anyone had seen in a very long time. And in her upraised hand was the reason for her smile: two large rabbits.

For a moment, no one spoke. *Had mother gone hunting so early in the morning?* Samantha wondered. *I didn't hear any gunshots.* At first, Chantal wanted to touch the animals. Perhaps she thought they were alive and she might play with them, but Samantha knew by the still, glassy eyes that these would not be pets.

The older girls had lived in the woods long enough to know few people could afford the luxury of keeping a rabbit as a pet. And sadly, sometimes even much-loved dogs and cats, who had important jobs on a farm, just disappeared— like their old dog Rover had a long time ago.

These rabbits meant they'd have meat to eat for the first time in a long while, and their mother knew how to make a delicious rabbit stew. Now she wasn't the only one with a big smile on her face!

"Girls, we have received a wondrous gift. These rabbits are like a blessing from heaven."

"A gift? From who?" Briar was curious.

"Well now, that's a bit of a mystery. I was sitting on the stump by the door, and I'd closed my eyes for a second or two, just thinking about a great many things and listening to the birds. Then when I stood up to come in, I spotted these lying on one of those flat rocks near the edge of the clearing. They almost looked like an offering someone had placed on an altar. I didn't know what to think, and I looked around to see if anyone was there."

"Was there?" Briar's soft whisper now sounded frightened.

"Yes. A man was standing in the trees. I could have easily missed him because he blended in and was silent. He really startled me!"

"It must have been a neighbour," Samantha suggested. "Didn't you recognize him?" They had very few neighbours, and most of them lived at least a mile or two away, so they didn't see them very often.

"He certainly wasn't a neighbour, or at least not one we know. He was a native man, but he wore a white man's clothes. He didn't speak, as I said. I had the impression he was just waiting to make sure I saw the rabbits, and then he left. I wish I'd been quicker to say thank you."

She walked over to the table and laid the rabbits down. Chantal ran over to touch them, but suddenly became shy and put her hand out timidly to stroke their soft fur.

"Soft bunny," she said.

"Yes," Mother agreed. Then she began singing a nursery rhyme.

> *"Bye, baby Bunting*
> *Father's gone a-hunting*
> *Gone to get a little rabbit skin*
> *To wrap his baby Bunting in."*

She stopped just as suddenly as she'd begun, and her smile disappeared. *She's probably thinking of Father,* Samantha thought.

"I wish I'd been quicker to realize what a gift he's given us and say thank you," Mother repeated. "But he disappeared. Perhaps someday we'll see him again, and then we can tell him how grateful we were."

Briar's blue eyes were huge. "Do you think there are more Indians around, Mama? What if he comes back and brings more Indians with him? What will we do?"

"I don't imagine there's anything to fear. He has only shown us an act of kindness. And we've never heard any stories of unfriendly Indians around here, have we?"

"We've hardly ever seen an Indian," Samantha chimed in. "But the ones we did see looked about as poor as we are and didn't seem scary."

"I'm scared," Chantal cried, huddling closer to her mother. Mother stroked her curly head and tried to soothe her. "For now, we should just be thankful that we'll enjoy a delicious rabbit stew for a few days. You can help me pull some vegetables from the garden, if the other rabbits have left us any. Maybe that's how these two got so nice and plump! We were fattening them up all along, and we just didn't know it!"

That thought made everyone smile, even Chantal.

CHAPTER SIX

Rabbit Stew and Visitors Too

After breakfast, Mother took the rabbits outside to skin and clean on a tree stump. Without their fluffy fur, they didn't look as big, but everyone was excited about having a superb stew that night—except for Chantal, who had thought they might be pets.

Fighting swarms of bloodthirsty mosquitoes, Samantha and Briar made their way to the stream for buckets of cold water. One would be for filling the wash basin perched on a stump outside the door. The morning air still felt fresh, but it was going to be another scorcher. They'd need the other buckets just for drinking and cooling off.

After everyone's morning wash-up, it was time to do some weeding in the garden, feed Bonnie, brush her down, and put her in the little pasture, where her tail was in constant motion swatting away mosquitoes. Next, they'd feed the rooster and chickens, gather any eggs, wash them off, and clean out the smelly henhouse. Only then would there be time to play.

It was bread-making day for Mother, and already the sweet, yeasty aroma of rising dough filled the cabin. They also heard something quite new today: happy humming. The stranger's gift had truly lifted Mother's spirits.

Playing usually meant playing school. The girls took turns being the teacher and enjoyed coming up with lessons for their pretend students. The students either sat on the grass or on two stumps, and the teacher stood, using a long pointed stick to draw figures or words on the ground.

There were four books in their home: a large, heavy Bible, a small volume of poetry, a map-filled geography book, and another filled with paintings of beautiful birds. From this modest library, Mother taught a lesson most evenings, and they were gaining quite a useful store of information. Even Chantal was quickly grasping her alphabet.

"What is two plus five?" Teacher Briar asked today, beginning with arithmetic.

"Fifteen!" shouted Chantal delightedly, swatting away some pesky mosquitoes with a leafy branch.

"Not quite." Briar smiled. Then she broke up some twigs into even-sized pieces and laid two and then five of them side by side on the ground. "Now count them carefully. I'll be back to you in a minute."

Turning to her big sister, she asked her to recite the poem *Ozymandias*, one of their father's favourites. Samantha stood tall, pretending she faced an audience, and in a clear voice spoke.

> "I met a traveller from an antique land
> Who said: 'Two vast and trunkless legs of stone
> Stand in the desert . . . '"

Although they didn't quite understand its meaning, this poem about a fallen statue in Egypt was mysterious and mystical, and both girls enjoyed it as much as their father had. It also reminded them of him and, while it often stirred their sadness and sense of loss, they somehow felt a deeper connection to him by reading it.

"I miss school," Samantha said to Briar. "Don't you?"

"Yes, but I don't remember much about it," Briar replied. "I hope a new teacher comes soon."

"So do I. Everybody does, especially Mother. She wants us all to have a good education, and I want to be a real teacher someday, not just a pretend one when we play school."

"I do remember how far away school is," Briar said. "It's almost too far for us to walk, and Chantal will be ready to start soon. It's not a problem for some of the other kids because they live closer to the village."

"I know," Samantha said with a sigh. Then she brightened. "Do you remember the winter Father made skis for us to get to school? He hammered and hammered at some old barrel staves until they turned into skis! It was like magic!"

"I remember," said Briar. "But we could only ski on good days. There were lots of icy days when we had to stay home."

"Some snowy days Father hitched Bonnie to the cutter. That was fun. But I guess we can't do that anymore."

Samantha thought about the horse-drawn cutter in which Father or Caleb had sometimes driven them through the snow. It had fallen into disrepair when their father became ill. *Old Bonnie is still in good shape, though. She might be able to carry the three of us on her back on nasty weather days, but she might stumble and injure herself. And it would be really cruel to leave her tied to the hitching post outside school all day in snow and freezing rain.*

"Well, we don't have to worry about that right now, since there isn't any school!" she reminded Briar.

Samantha knew Briar missed their father tremendously, just as she did. Although Chantal barely remembered him, it was obvious to Samantha that her youngest sister felt his absence and the worry and tension in their home since his death. The older girls, when out of their mother's hearing, often talked and worried about their missing brother too. Since it upset their mother to speak of him, they didn't in her presence.

Like most big brothers, Caleb had been a huge tease. Many times they'd told him they wished he'd just go away and leave them alone, but when he actually did, it was a different matter. Then the girls felt guilty and sorry they'd ever wished it. *If only I could take back some of the things I said!* Samantha thought. *Oh, Caleb. I didn't mean any of it.*

Now that two years had passed, she no longer expected him to return; she just worried almost constantly about what might have happened. Had he had an accident? Was he hurt and alone? Had someone taken him in? Sometimes she would try to have more positive thoughts: maybe he was working on another farm somewhere. Maybe he'd found a place where there were more young people his age and more opportunities to save some money from his wages.

"Seven!" Chantal exclaimed suddenly with a proud smile.

"Excellent!" Teacher Briar enthused. "You shall receive a star today, Chantal." And with that, she picked up a piece of charcoal from an old campfire and drew a tiny black star on the back of the little girl's hand.

They were just beginning to clap for her when a deep, menacing growl startled them.

CHAPTER SEVEN

Two Fierce Mothers

Chantal shrieked. Briar screamed, "Mama!"

Samantha darted sideways and, scooping up Chantal, hissed to Briar, "Keep quiet and stand still!"

The pungent scent of the skinned rabbits had caught the attention of the black bear, and she came thrashing through the woods, two thin cubs running behind her, heading straight for them. In the field, a terrified Bonnie caught the bears' scent and whinnied wildly. With her eyes half on the mother bear and half on the house, Samantha saw her mother tear open the cabin door, take in the frightening scene, and reach for the loaded shotgun hanging above the door. She caught the look of horror on Mother's face and noted her shaking hands and the visible effort to calm herself.

Mother managed to whisper to the girls to back up slowly toward the cabin.

The ravenous mother bear was halfway across the clearing. Mother held her breath to steady her hands. The girls squeezed their eyes shut. When the gun fired, the explosion shook the woods. At first, no one could hear. Samantha waited for the sound of the bear falling but heard nothing; she could certainly smell her musky odour, though! Peeking through her fingers, she was almost afraid to look. For a moment, the bear stopped and looked behind for her cubs. Their frantic, terrified squeals enraged her, and she began to charge again. Mother fired once more, this time nipping a paw. The bear emitted a strange, bawling sound, almost like that of a sheep. Dripping blood, she hightailed it into the woods, her squealing cubs at her heels, tumbling over each other in their haste.

After the blast of the shotgun and her momentary deafness, a stunned Samantha realized her whole body was trembling. Briar and Chantal were running to their mother, but Samantha was unable to move. After what felt like forever, but was probably only a few seconds, she took one step, then another, and slowly advanced toward her mother, as if in a trance.

Placing the heavy gun on the ground, Mother rushed forward, arms open, to enfold them all. She was trembling too, and sobbing quietly. "Oh, my dears, my dears!" she cried in a trembling voice. "I'm so sorry. I should never have left the rabbits out there to tempt that poor bear."

"Why do you call him a poor bear?" asked Chantal, whose eyes were still wide with fright.

After taking a moment to breathe slowly and calm herself, Mother attempted a reassuring smile and answered, "Because she's not a 'him'—she's a mother, just like I am. She's trying to look after her babies, trying to find food for them. It's too bad I had to wound her, but I had no choice. I had to protect my babies."

"Maybe her paw will heal and she'll find some fish in the stream," Briar said. "I hope so. But all the same, I was really, really scared, Mama."

"So was I," Samantha whispered. A tear rolled down her cheek, and she hugged her mother more tightly.

"Not me—I wasn't scared at all!" said Chantal.

***

Later that evening, before they dipped into the aromatic stew, Mother said a special grace. She gave thanks for the man who had brought the rabbits to them, and for the fact that the bear hadn't harmed her family. Then, as she'd heard about a native custom of thanking the spirit of the animal they were about to eat, she thanked the rabbits for the strength and nourishment her children were about to receive from their meal.

Everyone said, "Amen!" but a sombre Samantha couldn't stop thinking, *That was really a close call! What would have happened if Mother's shot had missed? And what if the bear comes back?*

CHAPTER EIGHT

Danger in the Woods

While Samantha lay in bed worrying about where her brother could be, Caleb paused in his journey to breathe in the freshness of the new day. He'd only been on the road for an hour, but his hungry body was already protesting. In contrast, his spirit was as joyful as the chorus of morning birdsong that surrounded him in the woods. Every step brought him closer to home. He could almost feel its nearness today. By his calculations, he was a just an hour or two north of the village of Huntsville.

Last night, he had slept out under the stars again. He'd done that most nights on this journey, usually so tired he fell into an immediate deep sleep the moment he stretched out. Some nights, though, sleep didn't come easily, and he'd study the sky, recalling the names of some of the constellations he recognized as if they were old friends. When he did sleep, the howls of nearby wolves and strange rustlings in the bush often interrupted his rest. But only two creatures had ever actually attacked: bloodthirsty blackflies and menacing mosquitoes. In addition, even on a warm night, sleeping on the grass meant waking up damp and chilled from the morning dew. So whenever he found a barn or shed, he'd slip in unseen and find a cozier place to bed down. So far, he'd been lucky; no one had discovered him. A few times, guided by "the poor man's lantern," the moon, he'd walked late into the night in light so bright, it was as if a million candles lit up the countryside.

The supply of bannock bread he'd started out with was long gone, and he usually dined on what berries he could find, but one lucky day he had actually managed to catch a small trout. His mouth began to water just thinking of that feast. Now he was constantly famished and knew he couldn't go on much longer without proper nourishment.

Caleb had met few travellers on his route since leaving Sudbury. They were either nervous of strangers and didn't speak or just gave a friendly nod and passed by. Once, a family had shared their lunch with him and asked many questions about where he'd been and where he was going. They were intrigued by Caleb's adventure, and it had been pleasant sitting in the pasture beside the trail with them. He was sorry when they'd had to part.

He was thankful for this morning's blessedly cool shade. However, in that shade, the mosquitoes were even more aggressive than usual, and he'd scratched himself raw in places. He'd already accumulated plenty of bites as he travelled, but now his hands were dotted with specks of dried blood, and he assumed his neck and face were too. He really hated it when the annoying insects got into his hair; he'd scratch his scalp until it sometimes bled as well. Worst of all was when they swarmed his face and he swallowed one or two by accident! Yuck! It made him gag.

The route began to follow the shore of a narrow river, and Caleb left the road to wade in up to his knees. Splashing his face and arms with the cool water felt blissful. He leaned way over, submerged his entire head, and lifting it out, shook his hair from side to side with abandon, like a shaggy dog spraying a vast arc of water droplets that would have soaked anyone standing nearby. The cool water soothed his bites, and he scooped up delicious handfuls to gulp down. He felt refreshed and revived as he hurried back to the road, which led deeper into the bush.

An hour later, Caleb thought, *Shouldn't be long now till I start seeing some cabins on the outskirts of Huntsville.* When the road turned and bordered the river again, he decided it was time for another cold drink. The morning's freshness was waning, and the singing of heat bugs foretold another scorching day.

After pushing through some low, scrubby bushes, Caleb emerged near the river's edge and spied two boys standing in the water with fishing lines. They were so absorbed in what they were doing, they didn't hear his approach, and he took a moment to observe them. A lanky fellow with dark, unruly hair that fell over his eyes looked to be about his age, while the other boy, a freckled short redhead, seemed a couple of years younger. As Caleb approached, he noticed a heavily laden canoe pulled up on shore beside the boys, a carelessly placed shotgun resting on its gunnels. Fine tendrils of smoke rose from a campfire that had recently been doused with water. Caleb guessed the boys had been sent to Huntsville to pick up supplies for their family and had camped here overnight.

"Morning!" he called out in a friendly fashion. The startled boys turned and scowled at him but said nothing. He waited a moment or two for some kind of response, but the two were not inclined to talk; their faces remained sullen and unfriendly.

Despite their hostility, Caleb decided to ask a couple of questions about the route and distances. The freckled redhead glanced sideways at his companion, as if seeking permission to answer Caleb's questions. The tall boy's eventual nod was so slight, it was barely noticeable. Both boys kept their eyes on him, while the redhead muttered a terse reply. Based on this brief answer, Caleb made some swift calculations in his head, confirming what he'd already been thinking.

"Looks like I've got about two more days ahead of me, maybe a day and a half, if I'm lucky."

There was no response again.

Finally, the taller boy spoke. "You say you're headin' to the south shore o' Lake o' Bays?"

"Near there," Caleb replied, surprised by this sudden response.

"Might save yourself a day's walk if you got a few pennies extra," the boy said, smirking. Then he and his friend looked at each other and chuckled, as if the thought of Caleb having a few extra pennies was funny.

"How's that?" At first Caleb thought they were going to offer him a ride. He wouldn't have minded one, but the canoe was already so loaded that it would sit low in the water. There clearly wasn't room for a passenger. Besides, the boys were probably headed in the opposite direction.

Now the younger boy, whom Caleb mentally dubbed Red, became quite animated and shared some startling news. "There's this new boat crossin' Lake of Bays. She's steam-powered. Carries passengers and supplies. Saves a lot of time." His eyes flashed with excitement; he was obviously impressed by the size and capabilities of the boat. Red turned to the other boy, who Caleb thought of as Slim, as if seeking confirmation of his opinion.

Caleb was tempted by the adventure of being on board such a ship and how wonderful it would be to arrive home faster. "I've never seen anything like that! Sounds amazing. Have you been on it?"

Before Red could answer, Slim gave Caleb a sly, sidelong look. Caleb noticed he was edging a little closer to the canoe and the shotgun when he said, "Nah. It ain't cheap. You got the fare for something like that?"

Caleb became acutely aware of his meagre savings hidden in the sock wrapped around his waistband. He'd almost forgotten about it this morning. Suddenly, he felt its weight, and he thought surely the boys would notice the slight bulge under his thin shirt. He prayed it was baggy enough to cover the bulge well.

Hoping his face wouldn't betray his nervousness, Caleb put on a smile and tried to joke. "Heck, no! Do I look like someone who can afford to ride around on a fancy boat? It's been days since I even had a good meal!"

He must have been convincing, because Red looked him over from head to toe and laughed. "You look even worse off than us."

Slim stared at Caleb for a long moment, looking uncertain whether or not to believe him. Then he seemed to arrive at some conclusion and, reaching down into the canoe with his free hand, picked up the shotgun.

Caleb froze. Were they going to search him and find his money? Damn! He was so close to home, and to think he might lose his savings now, after keeping them safe for so long, was infuriating. *Well, they're not going to get them!* Hot anger rose in his throat. He had to get away from these two. *Think of something! And fast!*

CHAPTER NINE

A Strange Turn of Events

Caleb could not believe what was happening. These two boys must have decided he had something worth stealing after all. The flush of anger rushing through his body was accompanied by an icy fear and a trembling in his legs. *Stay calm!* he thought. *Stay calm! Easy to say! They look nervous. No telling what a nervous person pointing a gun at you might do.* His fingers itched to pat his hidden money reassuringly, but he knew that would be a dead giveaway.

Slim moved to stand in front of his canoe; Red laid down his fishing rod and stood beside him, staring at Caleb as if daring him to try something.

"Whoa, there! Hold on! I told you I don't have anything!"

"Yeah, and you're not getting any o' this here, either," shouted Slim, pointing the gun directly at Caleb.

It took a moment for Caleb to see through the red haze of his warring emotions and understand what Slim was saying. *They aren't going to rob me! They're afraid I'll rob them!* This was such a crazy turn of events that he would have laughed if Slim hadn't been pointing the gun at him. He hoped the boys' nervousness wouldn't make them careless with it. It was time to get out of this situation, if he could, before it became any worse.

"Hey, put the gun down!" he said in a shaky voice. "You've got it all wrong. I don't want your stuff. I just stopped to be friendly." He hoped he sounded convincing. He couldn't tell by watching their faces whether or not they believed him; all he saw was anger and perhaps a hint of fear in their eyes as well.

"You better hit the road," Red shouted, trying to sound menacing. He wasn't scary, but the gun sure was.

"All right, I'm going. Maybe I'll get lucky and see that boat when I get near the lake." Pointing at their fishing rods, Caleb added, "Hope you catch a big one."

Holding his breath, he tried to calm his heart as he backed up with great care, his eyes still on the gun. Then he turned and raced back toward the road. He wanted to look back and make sure he wasn't being followed but didn't dare chance it. All the while, he waited for the crack of a gunshot. Thankfully, it never came.

When he felt sure he'd put a safe distance between himself and the boys, Caleb allowed himself to slow down. Bit by bit, his heart returned to its normal beat, but he was soaked in sweat. Instinctively, he touched the sock strapped to his waist, reassuring himself that all was well.

That was close! I can't believe it! Here I was, scared they were going to rob me, and all that time they thought I was going to rob them! He chuckled bitterly.

His thoughts returned to what they had said about the new steamship. He knew Lake of Bays was vast, and that it took several days to walk all the way around it. The idea of taking the ship was tempting. He could probably board in Huntsville, but in the end, even though it meant he could get home a day or two faster, he was unable to bring himself to part with one penny of his treasure.

Caleb decided he just had to keep putting one foot in front of the other. *Shank's mare is good enough for me!* he thought, remembering that funny old Irish term for walking that his father sometimes used. Closing his eyes briefly, he brought his father's smiling face into focus. Then he imagined that deep, encouraging voice saying, as it so often did, "No need to hitch up the wagon, Caleb. We'll go shank's mare!"

Father! Caleb sighed. *I never thought I'd miss you and the family so much! I just hope you'll be glad to see me again.* Whatever the future held for him, he wanted only to be with his family right now. No matter how tough the situation might be at home, he was determined to make the best of it. After two years of fending for himself, one thing had become very clear: life wasn't easy anywhere. He'd been lonelier than he would have believed possible.

Whatever you want me to do—work on the farm, or in the lumber camp—I'll do it. Just give me the chance!

Stop thinking! he finally thought. *Just keep putting one foot in front of the other.*

And then Caleb let out a big whoop of pure joy. He was relieved that the boys fishing on the river hadn't insisted on searching him, and he was relieved to be so much closer to home. Picking up his pace, he began singing one of his marching songs again.

> "The grand old Duke of York,
> He had ten thousand men,
> He marched them up to the top of the hill,
> Then marched them down again."

CHAPTER TEN

Almost Home

The longer days at this time of year were allowing Caleb to make good progress. But now the setting sun splashed the sky with hues of orange and red, warning it would soon be dark. *I'll have to find somewhere to sleep soon.*

With luck this'll be my last night. Tomorrow, I should be home.

Home! The more he thought about it, the more mixed emotions he felt: hope and longing, apprehension and worry. He'd become very homesick. Strange when he remembered how much he'd wanted to leave two years ago.

Caleb knew his parents would want to know why he'd run away, and for days he'd been struggling to find the right words. *Maybe there aren't any.* Still, he tried. His mind ran through various explanations that might help them understand, but he shook his head in frustration. There was no simple answer; his reasons were complicated.

I was just plain tired—that's what it was. He couldn't think of another way to describe how he'd felt. *We worked from sun-up to sundown, clearing the land and putting in crops and everything, then we'd fall into bed exhausted and get up and start all over again the next day. Life seemed to be nothing but work, work, work, all the time.* He remembered feeling there would never be an end to it. He also remembered days when there hadn't been enough to eat and his stomach had growled all night long.

And then that last winter, when Father took me with him to the lumber camp . . . the cold was brutal. One morning he and several others had woken to discover the clothes they were sleeping in had frozen to the icy walls beside their bunks! The memory made him shiver, even though he was sweating on this sweltering day.

But there had been some happy times; he smiled, remembering a couple of friends from school, Barry and Peter. They'd shared jokes and played great pranks on some of the other boys. Their school days were cut short, however; each of them was needed at home. Barry and his father had gone to the lumber camp with Caleb and his father that last winter Caleb was home.

Caleb sometimes missed those days of carefree fun when he'd still been in school, and now he wondered if Barry and Peter had missed them too. Before long he'd become restless at home and then angry too. The daily drudgery wore him down. *I wanted something to happen, but I didn't know what. Sure couldn't tell anybody how I felt. Didn't know what to say.*

It was shortly after returning from that winter in the lumber camp that he'd walked away from it all. *Guess I thought if I left there'd be one less mouth to feed, one less person to worry about.* Caleb shook his head. What a mistake that had been! *What did I know? Probably all they did was worry about me after I'd gone.*

Caleb's thoughts returned to the present. He was fifteen now and he'd seen a bit of life. He believed he'd grown "in wisdom and in stature," as the good book said, or so he hoped. He also hoped his father would recognize that change in him and welcome him back.

To many people, he was now an adult, ready to take on a man's responsibilities, including a man's work. He had worked like a man, hard, physical labour, which had built his muscles and strengthened him. He had thought the lumber camp was tough, but he now knew that life in a Sudbury nickel mine, which was where he'd ended up, was even tougher and more dangerous. No, he was more than ready for an aboveground existence again.

Maybe Father and I can clear another field and try planting some corn and potatoes again. We lost the last crop, but it's worth another try . . . if they'll let me stay, that is.

***

A small clearing appeared; someone was trying to open up a field for grazing or planting. Stumps of felled trees dotted the area, and random clumps of long grass sprouted from the earth. Caleb knew there would be a homestead nearby. If there was a barn to sleep in, it would be ideal, but even if there wasn't it was time to stop for the night. Skirting the clearing, he discovered a worn path leading away from the road, presumably toward a cabin. He followed it, passing through brush almost tall enough to conceal him. Not wanting to be seen, he was on full alert, listening for voices or other sounds of habitation. A dog would be bad news, so he prayed there wasn't one. All he could hear were buzzing insects.

Turning a bend, he tripped on a root and fell flat on his face, letting out a little surprised "Ooof!" Sharp pains shot through his sprained knee, and he was furious with himself for being so careless. As he stood and brushed his filthy trousers, he caught a movement out of the corner of his eye: a large brown-and-white Jersey cow was staring mournfully at him. He noted a tall girl peeping over the cow's flank and staring. Before he could speak, she abandoned the cow and ran in the opposite direction, yelling, "Pa! Pa! Help! He-e-e-lp!"

"Sorry! I didn't mean to scare you!" Caleb shouted after her, but she wasn't listening. "Damn!" Now he could hear a dog barking somewhere nearby.

He started to retrace his steps quickly, but his knee really slowed him down. *Great. Just what I needed. I should have been watching where I was going.* Moments later, an old collie was madly running circles around him, barking fiercely and neatly corralling him.

"Stop right there!" bellowed a very deep voice. Caleb turned to face a small man pointing a large gun straight at him. One angry eye squinted down the barrel of the weapon while the other glared at him. Under his weathered hat, the man's grizzled face looked fierce.

"Sorry! I'm sorry, sir. I didn't mean to frighten anyone, honest! I don't want to cause any trouble. I'll just take my leave, if you'll let me." He was shaking and upset with himself for showing such fear, but he certainly felt afraid. All the time he was talking he couldn't take his eyes off the shotgun. Only that morning Slim had pointed his weapon at him! Once again he reminded himself, *Try to stay calm!*

The deep voice thundered, "Who are ya? What're ya doing here? Did ya think you were goin' to get away with one o' my chickens? If that's what yer after, you'll be sorry! I'm losin' enough of 'em to the wolves and foxes. Darn thievin' animals!"

"No, sir. I don't want your chickens. I didn't even know you had any! I was just looking for a bit of shelter for the night." He kept a wary eye on the still circling and barking dog.

"Charlie, off!" the man shouted. Charlie obediently moved away and sat at his master's heels. Quivering with excitement, he gave one last sharp bark, as if to show he was still on guard.

"Haven't told me who ya are yet, or what yer doin' here."

"I'm Caleb Lawson, sir. My folks have a cabin about a few miles east, and I'm trying to get home. I've been travelling for a couple of weeks and I'm really tired. This should be my last night." He pleaded, "I just want to get home tomorrow, sir."

The man still pointed the gun at him. "Lawson, eh? Heard of 'em, but I only heard of some little girls. Went to the school with my girl. Never heard of a boy. You lyin' to me?"

"No, sir. I swear. I've been gone two years. Worked my way up to Sudbury. Got a job in a new mine. Now I just want to see my family again." Suddenly, he had a thought. "If your daughter went to school with my sisters, I can prove who I am. Their names are Samantha, Briar, and Chantal Lawson. My father is Jarvis Lawson."

The small man lowered the gun a bit. His wary eyes assessed Caleb for a few moments, which seemed an eternity. Then he said, "Well, it'll be dark soon. Guess ya can spend a night in the barn. But make sure yer gone by dawn! I don't want ya lingerin' around here any longer than that. And if ya go after my chickens, I'll hear 'em squawkin' and I'll be back, and not without this gun!"

"No, sir. Thank you, sir. Thank you. I won't linger. I want to get home tomorrow."

"All right. Walk ahead of me now, and I'll show ya to the barn."

"Thank you, sir," Caleb repeated gratefully.

As they started off, a tall young man approached. He was making an effort to move quickly, but he walked with difficulty, and his handsome face, rather than displaying the smoothness of youth, revealed deep lines drawn there by a pain his eyes could not hide.

"What's going on, Pa? Who's this?" he demanded.

"Everything's fine, Andrew. This'un says he's a Lawson. Says it's his family lives a bit down the road. Asked if he could put up in the barn overnight. Don't see no harm in that, long as he behaves hisself. No need to stir yerself about it. You can go back to the house now."

The young man looked hurt by his father's dismissal but attempted not to show it. Instead, he turned on Caleb.

"What're you doing, sneaking around here? If you were an honest person, you'd have come to the door and asked for help, not scared my sister half to death."

"Sorry. I didn't know she was there, and I didn't mean to cause any trouble. I just didn't see any harm in putting up in a barn for one night."

"Oh, you didn't? Well, if it was up to me, you'd be on your way. How do we know you're really who you say you are, anyway?"

"That's enough, son!" The older man's voice was harsh. "I've got things well in hand." Turning to Caleb, he nodded to indicate they should proceed toward the barn.

The young man shot a malevolent glance at Caleb and angrily turned back to the house, moving awkwardly again. Caleb tried not to stare after him. Although he hadn't appreciated the fellow's manner toward him, he did feel some sympathy; the farmer had spoken very sharply to his son and embarrassed him in front of a stranger.

The barn was little more than a lean-to with room for the cow he'd just seen and an old mare who watched him with interest. The farmer pointed to a mound of hay in one corner. "You can spread a bit o' that out to lie on, if ya want."

"Thank you, Mr. . ." Caleb realized he didn't know the man's name.

"Thank you, sir."

"Name's Whylie."

"Then thank you, Mr. Whylie," Caleb said, offering up a nervous smile.

The man did not return his smile. Instead he looked around his small barn as if assessing the situation, and appearing satisfied, nodded to Caleb and left without another word.

Caleb noticed a wooden trough by the two stalls and lowered his face into the water, which although a bit warm to be refreshing, still quenched his thirst and felt wonderful on his dusty face.

He arranged a comfortable thickness of fresh hay on the dirt floor, covering it with a worn and ratty horse blanket. All the while, his stomach rumbled from lack of food. But fatigue quickly overwhelmed him, and he was asleep almost before he lay his head down.

His dream that night was all about food: fresh bread, roast chicken, apple pie with cream, and all sorts of other delights. It was so real, he could smell the new bread and the crispy chicken. He was just about to start in on a cinnamon-laced slice of pie when he awoke. The enticing aroma was still present. Looking around, he saw a nervous tiny woman standing at the barn door. The farmer stood behind her, still carrying that big gun. In the woman's hands was a steaming plate of food.

"My wife's got too soft a heart. She wouldn't listen to me and let ya be. Had to bring ya somethin' to eat."

"If you're telling the truth and you're the Lawson boy," the woman said quietly, "it's the least I can do. Even if you aren't telling the truth, it isn't in me to let anybody go hungry." She handed Caleb the plate of chicken and potatoes.

Caleb was so grateful, he almost cried. He knew he was hungry, but he hadn't realized he was ravenous. He wanted to fall on the meal like a starving wolf, but he remembered his manners. "Thank you for your kindness, ma'am . . . Mrs. Whylie. It's been so long since I've eaten anything as tasty as this. I can't thank you enough. Wish I could repay the favour. Maybe someday I can."

"Don't you worry yourself about that," Mrs. Whylie replied, twisting her hands in her apron. "I hope if my boy were in the same kind of trouble, someone would help him." She turned and looked over her shoulder. Caleb followed her glance and spied the scowling young man, Andrew, lurking by the door.

As if annoyed at his mother's comment, Andrew spoke. "My mother said, 'If you're telling the truth.' How do we know you are? You told my father you'd been up in Sudbury working in a mine. Why should we believe you? For all we know, you've been in some kind of trouble, maybe even in jail."

Before Caleb even had a chance to retort, Mrs. Whylie scolded her son. "That's enough, Andrew! I also said even if he *wasn't* telling the truth, I couldn't let him go hungry, and it's not up to us to judge."

Turning back to Caleb, she added, "Now eat up, young man, and I wish you well tomorrow."

"Thank you, ma'am."

He thought, *I need all the good wishes I can get.*

Then he hungrily attacked the chicken dinner.

CHAPTER ELEVEN

Andrew

Andrew watched as his mother said goodnight to Caleb, and his father gave
the boy a curt nod before leaving the barn. He was still annoyed that the kid
was being allowed to spend the night there but decided not to annoy his
mother by saying anything more. He simply shot one last malevolent look
at Caleb before following his parents back to the house. Although he lagged
behind, he was close enough to overhear his mother say, "Jim, you know Jarvis
Lawson passed away last year, but that boy doesn't seem to know. I gather
you hadn't told him, so I didn't say anything. When he finds out, he's in for a
terrible shock."

"True, but it wasn't our place to tell him," his father replied. "Good
thing he's come back, though—his mama and those girls must surely need help.
I guess he's gonna get quite the big welcome tomorrow. Now you stop worryin'
about that boy, Mother, and let's get to bed. Mornin' comes soon enough."

Looking back over her shoulder, his mother called, "Andrew, are you coming in now, son?"

In the rapidly failing light, she probably couldn't see the scowl on his face as he looked back at the barn and reluctantly replied, "Yeah, I'm coming, Ma."

***

Later that night, Andrew lay awake in the dark, listening. The utter quiet and stillness of the night was profound. Clouds obscured the stars, and no moonbeams slanted through the window. His parents and sister were long asleep, and the peace was only interrupted now and then by his father's light snoring.

None of the usual creaking sounds escaped from the house. There wasn't even a light breeze to stir the air in his room as he shifted his body again, trying to find a comfortable position on his mattress. He was weary and longed for the oblivion of sleep but knew it was unlikely to come soon. Shooting pains ripped through his back, and his bad leg twitched with a pulsating ache.

His mind was active, his brain unable to stop running through the day's events: that kid, Caleb Lawson, sneaking onto the property, scaring his sister, and getting Andrew's father all riled up. Something about Caleb grated on Andrew's nerves. At first he wasn't sure if the kid was lying or not, but the more he thought about him, the more he recalled one of the younger boys at the school a few years ago who resembled the kid. Because the boy was so much younger, though, Andrew had barely noticed him.

School! Those days seemed like another life now. Andrew didn't like to think about the accident that had changed his world so completely, so he tried to shut his mind off. His mother always told him to count sheep when he couldn't fall asleep. He wondered where that old idea had originated. It never worked for him.

Everyone said he was lucky to be alive, that it was a miracle. Andrew didn't feel that way; his dreams had been crushed along with his body. He longed to be back working on the farm, not just visiting from time to time on his day off, as he had been today. Tomorrow, he'd head back to his job at the general store. Everyone said he was lucky to have that job too, but Andrew didn't agree with that either. People always had something to say, but they had no idea what it was like to be him.

His busy mind churned, his thoughts returning to Caleb Lawson. Why hadn't his father just run the kid off their land? The image of his mother bringing him that hot meal annoyed Andrew. Why should that bother him so much? He certainly wasn't jealous, was he? Jealous of what? A scrawny kid? *He might be scrawny*, Andrew's treacherous mind whispered, *but he's able-bodied.* He tensed with anger and then gasped as another spasm of pain ripped through his body.

CHAPTER TWELVE

A Day of Surprises

Caleb awoke the following morning even before the crowing rooster welcomed the day. At first he was disoriented and couldn't figure out where he was. The first thing he did was feel for that sock sewn into his waistband. *Still there!* Then all the stunning events of the previous evening quickly came back to him. It was a lot to take in. He hadn't had so much excitement in such a short period of time for a very long while! It made him smile.

Standing up, he neatly folded the old horse blanket and went to the trough to splash water on his face and hair. He fervently wished there was more he could do to tidy himself up and be more presentable when he walked up the path to his home and saw his family again. *These clothes are filthy, and they stink worse than an outhouse!* What was left of his old shoes was tied together with string and constantly coming undone and needing to be tied over and over.

Could try some glue, but they're probably a lost cause, just fit for the scrap heap. Maybe Father has an old pair that'll fit me now. My feet sure have grown.

He turned to find the cow staring at him with those mournful eyes again. It was always hard to tell whether a cow was happy or sad, because its big eyes always looked sad regardless of the situation. As if to answer his thoughts, the cow began to softly low. Caleb went over to pat on the head and, in return, she nuzzled him softly.

Just then the girl he'd frightened and her father entered the barn together.

Caleb stepped back and said nervously, "I was just giving her a friendly pat, sir." He noticed with relief that Mr. Whylie did not carry his gun this morning.

"Time to put her out to pasture. You'll be on your way now?" It wasn't really a question—more like an order.

"Yes, sir. Right now! Thanks again for your help. I'll never forget it." Turning to the young girl, who he realized, now that he really looked at her, was probably almost his own age, he apologized for scaring her so badly the previous evening. She immediately blushed and quickly thrust a warm package into his hands. The aroma told him that inside were homemade biscuits. He peeked inside to confirm it, and steam arose from the flaky buns.

"I don't know what to say. You've all been so good to me."

Looking at the floor, she replied almost in a whisper, "Mama didn't want you travelling on an empty stomach."

"Your father said you go to school with my sisters."

Blushing even more, she nodded, then said, "When there was school. There hasn't been for over a year since Teacher left. I haven't seen your sisters for a while."

"Well, I'll tell them I met you. What's your name?"

Before she could answer, her father put in, "She's Elsie May, but she don't like the name her good mama gave her. Just wants to be called May." He snorted with disgust, and the embarrassed girl looked away.

"I'll tell them I met you, May," Caleb said. Saying his goodbyes again, he walked out of the barn, the warm biscuits tucked under his arm.

As he headed across the stumpy meadow to reach the road,

Mr. Whylie suddenly bellowed after him, "Just hold on a minute there!" Predictably, Charlie's furious barking started up again.

Caleb froze, wondering if the farmer was going to cause trouble for some reason. "Yes, sir?" he asked, turning toward the man. Just as he'd done the night before, Charlie whipped around his legs in tight circles, still barking. "Nice dog, nice dog," a nervous Caleb kept repeating. In the distance, he spied Andrew, standing in the barnyard and staring at him.

Ordering the dog off, Mr. Whylie looked at Caleb. "You fit to do a bit o' work with that injured knee o' yers?"

Caleb was dumbfounded. This was the last thing he expected. For a moment, he didn't know what to say. Finally, he found his voice and answered with some hesitation. "Yes, sir. It should be fine in no time. Do you need help with something right now?" He hoped the man didn't, at least not right now. He was anxious to be on his way.

"Not right now. Maybe in a week or two. Startin' to fall a bit behind around here." A pained look crossed his face. "Never thought I'd need to hire help, but my boy can't do much anymore. Got injured at the lumber camp last winter." He paused, cleared his throat, and spat on the ground. "Damn lumber camps. Some of the men get hurt so bad they aren't good for much of anythin' anymore."

Well, that explains some of Andrew's behaviour, thought Caleb.

The man added, "Anyway, the boy's got some light work at the general store, and the girl isn't strong enough for much. Need a young fella."

"Sorry about your son. My father and I used to work in a camp near Baysville. I've seen some pretty bad accidents. It's not for me, if I can help it. But if we have to go back, I guess we'll have to go back. I'm not looking forward to it, though." *Why am I babbling on like this?* he thought. *I just want to get going! Must be because this fellow makes me nervous.*

"Well, I can likely give ya two days work a week, if yer interested. Maybe three. Can't pay much. Give ya yer meals and a place to sleep while yer here. You can go home for the rest o' the week. Might want to think about it or talk it over with yer fath . . . your family."

Caleb was quite excited at the opportunity this strange man was now giving him after threatening him with a shotgun just the night before. *With luck, that Andrew will be working in the village most of the time and I won't have to deal with him. But beggars can't be choosers.*

"I'd like that very much, sir. Thank you. I'll talk it over with my folks, but I'm sure they'll appreciate it too. I'll be back in a few days to let you know for sure. Thank you again, sir."

Mr. Whylie just nodded and turned back to his barn and his chores. Andrew was no longer in sight. Smiling broadly, Caleb turned back to the path once more. More good news to take home.

The smile disappeared when Andrew loomed, scowling, in front of him on the road. The scowl seemed to be a permanent fixture. "You'd better not cause any trouble around here!" he said gruffly. "We don't need you. We can manage just fine without you."

"What have I done to offend you? I'm not going to cause any trouble. Your father offered me a job and I need one. Think I want to spoil that?"

"How do I know what you would or wouldn't do? We don't know if we can trust you. Just watch your step is all I'm saying. You might fool my parents, but I'll be watching you."

Caleb just stared at Andrew, then shook his head in disgust and walked past him.

He tried to put Andrew out of his mind as he continued his journey, but something about the young man nagged at him. *Whylie, that's the family's name. Andrew Whylie . . . school . . . the older boys . . .* Caleb slapped his forehead as the realization hit him. *That's it! How could I have forgotten?* When he'd been in school, more than two years ago, there were a couple of older boys who sometimes waited outside to walk their younger siblings home. They also enjoyed flirting with the older girls, which was probably the real reason they came. Andrew Whylie had been one of them. *But he looked so different then. Tall and strong and always joking. Nothing like this Andrew I just met. He's a bully now. Maybe that accident changed him. It's funny I don't remember May at all. She must have been there too. But if she's Samantha's age, I guess I wouldn't have been paying attention.* Caleb shook his head in amazement. *Andrew Whylie!* He could almost feel sorry for the fellow . . . almost.

The miles passed quickly, with only a quick drink from a cool, clear stream and the remainder of the biscuits for mid-morning, but as he approached the familiar terrain of his childhood, he grew more and more apprehensive and nervous. *What if they say I'm not welcome anymore?* He couldn't imagine his parents would actually turn him away, but they'd probably be very angry about his unexplained absence. "I'll just have to be ready to face whatever happens," he told himself, sounding braver than he actually felt.

***

Around noon, Caleb approached the familiar clearing and was engulfed in a fierce storm of emotions: homesickness, love, fear, anxiety, and more feeling he was unable to name. Suddenly shy again, he loitered in the trees around the perimeter. He thought he could make out a childish shriek of joy inside the cabin. *That's probably Chantal! They must be having an early lunch. Wish I'd saved three or four of those buns to share, but I wasn't thinking.*

Moving around to the back of the cabin, he came upon the lean-to and was thrilled to see dear old Bonnie again. Approaching her carefully, he whispered, "Hi, old Bonnie, you good old girl. Hi, Bonnie. Remember me? It's Caleb." As the mare turned her head toward him, he put his hand on her flank and began to softly sing to her.

> "My Bonnie lies over the ocean.
> My Bonnie lies over the sea.
> My Bonnie lies over the ocean.
> Oh, bring back my Bonnie to me."

Bonnie made a nickering sound, shaking her head and tossing her mane to let him know she did remember him. She let out a loud neigh, as if in celebration.

"Sh-h-h!" Caleb said. "Don't give me away yet, girl! I need a bit more time to get ready to say hello to my folks. It's going to be a shock to them to see me again, and I'm really scared."

***

They could hear Bonnie's neigh inside the cabin.

"Could it be the bear nosing around again?" Samantha asked her mother.

The other two girls put down their forks and stopped eating. "Oh, no. Not the bear!" cried Briar.

"Will it hurt Bonnie?" Chantal said, worried.

Mother didn't take time to answer. She was already at the door lifting the shotgun. Turning to the girls, she warned them to stay inside no matter what happened. "No matter what!" she repeated firmly. Then she went out the door.

Chantal sobbed. "I hate that bear! I hope Mama shoots her!"

"Sh-h-h!" Samantha reassured them."It probably isn't the bear at all. Bonnie was likely just startled by a chipmunk or a raccoon. You know how skittish she can be."

Then she thought, *I really hope that's all it is, and that Mother will be all right. What'll I do if there's serious trouble? I don't know how to use a gun . . .*

At that moment, she felt the weight of the world on her shoulders. How she missed her father and brother!

With a sad heart and a sudden flash of anger that took her by surprise, Samantha thought, *They should both be here with us, Father and Caleb. They should be here!*

Turning away from her sisters, she wiped her eyes with her sleeve so they wouldn't see her tears.

Then, disobeying her mother's strict order, she slipped out the door to follow her.

CHAPTER THIRTEEN

A Close Call

Samantha was just in time to see her mother kick off her shoes and tiptoe around the outside of the cabin, attempting to be as quiet as possible in the low brush. She couldn't tell how much noise Mother was making because of the pounding of her own heart, which got louder with every step. She watched her mother lift the shotgun to her shoulder, then stop and prepare to take aim, presumably at the black bear. Mother would have to wait until the bear was a good distance away from Bonnie before she fired; she couldn't take a chance on hitting the mare. Suddenly, Samantha felt a paralyzing fear; she wanted to continue following her mother and see what was out there, yet she couldn't watch any longer. Tearfully praying for her mother's safety, she remembered the order to stay inside, no matter what, and returned to her sisters.

Bonnie produced a low whinny again.

Oh, no! The bear's going to attack poor Bonnie!

In her mind's eye, Samantha could picture their mother approaching the lean-to, finger on the trigger, ready to pull it any second. Mother would be trying to calm her breathing so she could get off a good shot. Samantha found herself also trying to slow down her own panicky breathing. After a few moments, she realized she hadn't yet heard a shot. Maybe there was nothing there—no bear, nothing.

Bonnie probably was just spooked by a chipmunk or a raccoon after all, she thought. But she wasn't really convinced.

***

Caleb whispered goodbye to Bonnie and, planning to disappear back into the trees for a bit, started to slip out of the lean-to on tiptoes. Just as he put his first foot outside, he heard a shout. "Stop right there!" It was so unexpected that he jumped. *What the heck . . . ?* Then he realized, *That's my mother!*

Turning to face her, he cried, "Mother! It's me!" His mother stared, stupefied and unbelieving. She still pointed the gun at him, and she was shaking. She couldn't speak. He noticed her bare feet. *Why is she in bare feet? Why's she holding a gun? What did she think was happening out here? She must have heard Bonnie. Guess I really frightened her when I came out of the lean-to.*

"Mother, it's all right. It's me, Caleb. I'm home."

"Caleb?" she repeated uncomprehendingly. "Caleb?"

Then she dropped the gun and let out a sob. He approached her shyly, uncertain what to do. His mother rushed to throw her arms around him, laid her head on his chest, and sobbed even more deeply.

"Oh, Caleb. I might have shot you! I thought it was a bear. Oh, I'm so sorry."

"It's all right. Guess I scared you. I was going to come to see you in a little bit."

"Caleb," she kept repeating. "Oh, son. You're alive and well. After all this time. We never knew . . . We worried so. We prayed for you. Oh, Caleb, why?"

He couldn't answer that right away. "I don't know, Mother. It's kind of a long story."

"It's all right. All that matters is you're here now."

As if she'd just taken it all in, she leaned back and said, "You're so much taller! And look at those muscles! My goodness, son, you're almost a young man. But so thin!"

Caleb felt embarrassed and didn't know what to say. His mother smiled at him, and then as if suddenly remembering something, straightened herself, and tightly clasping his hand, led him forward. "Come inside. Your sisters are going to be so excited. They won't believe it. Oh, Caleb. *I* can't believe it! I'm so glad you're home!"

He was unable to speak; he had just heard the words he had longed for all through the weeks of his journey home. He walked eagerly toward the cabin.

CHAPTER FOURTEEN

Family Reunion

"Girls! Look who I've found!" Mother exclaimed excitedly. She was beaming with delight.

Looking past her at the tall, young man, Samantha and Briar took only two seconds to yell, "Caleb!" almost at the same instant. Leaping from their chairs, they rushed forward and threw their arms around him.

In their haste, the girls nearly knocked over Chantal. As Caleb laughed and hugged Samantha and Briar, he spotted his baby sister, looking alarmed.

"Mama!" she cried, raising her arms for a hug.

I was right. Chantal doesn't remember me, Caleb thought, and his heart ached. He watched his mother pick Chantal up and hug her. Then she whirled the child in a circle and said, "Darling, don't be afraid. Your big brother Caleb has come home at last. It's a miracle. Oh, yes, a true miracle."

Those words helped to ease Caleb's aching heart a little, but Chantal was still giving him a wary look. "The bad bear . . ." she muttered, looking confused.

"There was no bear, dear. It was only Caleb talking to old Bonnie out back. That's why she neighed! She was happy to see him too. Oh, it's just a miracle!" she repeated as she whirled Chantal around again in a little dance.

Caleb noticed Samantha and Briar glance at each other in amazement. He was just as surprised as they were; he hadn't ever seen his mother dance before! Chantal giggled, but as she was lowered to the floor she took refuge behind her mother's long skirt and peeked out at him. He gave her a big smile and winked.

Samantha and Briar were still hugging him so tightly, as if they never wanted to let go. With his arms around them, he began to laugh, even as they still had tears in their eyes.

"Help! I can't breathe!" he joked.

"Oh, Caleb! Where have you been?" Samantha cried, loosening her grip just a little.

Briar released him and stamped her foot. "Why did you go away?" she demanded.

Mother said, "Never mind the questions for now. Your poor brother is exhausted, and he must be hungry. He can answer your questions later, if he wants to. But I would like to hear some answers myself, so I hope he'll tell us all." She raised her eyes inquiringly at Caleb.

He nodded and said, "Where's Father? Out hunting or working? I hope he'll be as glad to see me as all of you." He was starting to get nervous again, wondering how Father would react when he saw him.

There was silence as everyone stared at him. Then Briar sobbed loudly and Samantha turned her face away. His mother looked stricken. Her face had gone pale, and she sat down heavily in a chair. She was just about to speak when Chantal blurted out, "Papa is in heaven. He doesn't live with us anymore."

"Oh, dear!" said his mother. "I wish I'd had a moment to prepare you for this news, Caleb. I'm so sorry. Father passed away a little over a year ago. Oh, son."

Stunned, Caleb felt as if all the blood were rushing from his head, and he felt suddenly faint. He began to sway. "Father's dead?" he whispered. His mother and Samantha rushed to grab him just as his knees buckled. They slowly lowered him into a chair at the table.

"Briar, fetch a cup of water from the bucket. Quickly, dear!" Mother said, and Briar hurried to comply.

Caleb appreciated the cool water. He sipped slowly, and Mother used her worn apron to wipe his face with some water. "There, there," she murmured. "You've had quite a shock. As have we all. There's been a lot for everyone to take in all of a sudden."

Soon everyone else sat down too, and looking around the table, Caleb could almost read their thoughts. It was as if each one contemplated the miracle of this reunion. He could see in their eyes that their hearts were filled with the joy of his return, and this touched him. Yet at the same time, he saw they were aching because there was one very important member of the family who would never return.

"How can he be dead?" Caleb asked. "What happened? Was it an accident?" His eyes searched his mother's, and in them he read her deep pain. Briar began to sob, and Mother drew her close to comfort her. "It must've been an accident! He wasn't old. He couldn't have just died!"

He felt terribly confused and disoriented. He had hoped for his father's forgiveness for running away, and now he felt lost and devastated. He would never see his father again, never hear his voice. He would never know whether or not he would have received that forgiveness.

"What happened?" he repeated.

"He just . . . just became worn out," his mother said in a soft voice. She paused as if to collect her thoughts. "I've thought about this over and over again. The farm was a huge disappointment for him. It was never going to be what he had hoped. Everything just finally took its toll on him, I think, and his heart gave out."

"I should've been here!" Caleb dropped his head into his hands. "I should've stayed. If I'd been here, he'd still be alive!"

"No! Oh, no, dear!" Her voice was fierce in its denial. Reaching across the table, she grabbed his hands. "Look at me!" she demanded. "Look at me!" Caleb lifted his eyes. He didn't think he could bear to see his mother's pain, believing he was the cause of it.

"Don't ever think that!" she said. "It was not your fault. It wasn't anyone's fault. If anything, it was the loss of his dream. Your father was a wonderful man, an idealist at heart, and perhaps he wasn't suited to this wild place. Perhaps neither of us was. But he loved it here, and he never gave up trying to make something of it."

"But I could have helped," Caleb protested. "And now I'll never be able to tell him I'm sorry." His eyes filled with tears again.

"Your father loved you dearly, son. You were his pride and joy. You would never have needed to say you were sorry. He would've been so happy to have you home again. I know that for certain. He would've thrown his arms around you." A slight smile appeared on her face. "He might even have danced with happiness, like I did!"

Caleb shook his head. He was still having difficulty absorbing everything his mother was saying. He looked at his sisters, each one strangely silent and still, and realized how much his reaction was disturbing them. They had been living with the loss of their father for some time, and he didn't want to upset them even more.

"Well," he said, trying to pull himself together, "maybe he would have hugged me, but I can't imagine him dancing!"

The tiny smile on Briar's face and the chuckle from Samantha were his reward. His mother patted his hand and smiled her appreciation.

CHAPTER FIFTEEN

Reality Sets In

"Do you think you could eat something now?" his mother asked Caleb after a while. "We have a delicious rabbit stew."

"I don't really feel like eating," he almost whispered. *How can I even think about food? Father is dead! Dead!* The word kept reverberating in his head.

"I know it's hard, son, but maybe you should have a little bit of something. You look so tired and thin."

He watched her rise from her chair and go to the stove, where she stirred a simmering pot. *I can't believe this. It doesn't seem real. All this time, I've been worrying about how he'd act when he saw me, and he hasn't even been alive! For more than a year. So Mother and the girls have been alone all this time.* Thinking about that made him feel even worse. *Yet they welcomed me with open arms. How could they? I don't deserve it.*

Mother put the steaming, fragrant bowl down in front of him, and the aroma revived him a bit. "Rabbit stew. Did you shoot it or set a trap?" He couldn't imagine his mother doing either.

"Neither. The rabbits were a sort of gift."

"From an Indian!" piped up Chantal. "I was scared, but Mama says he was a nice Indian."

"An Indian?" said Caleb, puzzled. "That's a strange thing."

"Yes, most unusual," replied Mother, "but most welcome too. We hadn't had any meat in quite a while." And she related the entire story.

"Well, that sure is something. I wonder if he knew you needed the help? Why was he wandering around here in the first place? Weren't you a bit scared too?"

"I was a bit at first, but then I realized what a kindness he had done for us, so I was just plain grateful. If I should ever see him again, I'll thank him from the bottom of my heart, but I don't suppose I will. But if he's one of Chief Big Wind's band, he probably hunts and fishes around here in the summertime, so it's possible."

Again, Caleb thought of his mother and the girls being alone here for over a year. They must have endured some very bad times. He was so glad he'd come back and only wished he'd done it sooner.

"Well, now that I'm back, I can hunt and trap. I might like to plant some crops too, in the field Father and I cleared. I know we didn't have much luck that last time, but I really want to try again."

He suddenly remembered Jim Whylie's offer of work on his farm. Turning to Samantha and Briar, he said, "I met a friend of yours yesterday. Elsie May Whylie, or just May, as she likes to be called."

Samantha's face lit up. "May Whylie! Oh, I haven't seen her in so long. She's a lot of fun. I wish they'd hurry up and find a new teacher soon so we can go back to school."

"Where did you see her?" asked Briar.

"Well, that's kind of a funny story. I'll tell you all the details later, but her father let me sleep in their barn last night, and her mother fed me a delicious chicken dinner. Then when I was leaving this morning, Mr. Whylie asked me if I'd like to help him out two or three days a week. He can't pay me much, but it would be something. I said I'd talk to you and . . . and . . . Father about it. Even a little bit of money would be a help around here, I imagine." Caleb dropped his eyes and stared at his hands. He was feeling lost at the idea of life without Father. His mother and sisters would be relying greatly on him now, and he worried he wouldn't be up to the task.

"That sounds like a good offer. Would you like to do that? We sure could use you around here too, but this sounds like an opportunity you should accept. Besides, you'd be here half the week, wouldn't you?" said Mother.

"Yes. I think I should accept the offer, but Mr. Whylie sure is a strange kind of man, pointing a gun at me one minute and offering me a job the next."

"A gun! Why on earth would he turn a gun on you? Oh, Caleb, are you sure you want to go back there? Would you be safe?"

"It's fine, Mother. I'll be perfectly safe. Mr. Whylie's harmless and Mrs. Whylie was nice. Their son's not very friendly, though—he seems quite resentful. Do you know anything about him?"

"I'm surprised to hear that. I see him in the store, but I don't really know him well. The poor fellow seems to be in a great deal of pain at times. He has a very difficult time getting around."

"Andrew used to be friendly. He was lots of fun," Samantha said, as if to defend him. "Sometimes May and I would meet him on the way home from school, and he'd give us each a ride on his shoulders. He had lots of funny riddles and stories too, but I guess that was before his accident."

"I'm sure he's a very nice young man, dear," Mother said to Samantha. Turning to her son, she added, "Caleb, this offer of work could be a real blessing, if you feel you'd be safe there."

"I do." Then he added, "Now put me to work here, Mother. Should I start on that wood that's piled up for splitting? Do you need water? What about Bonnie? Does she need turning out?"

"Slow down. There's plenty to do and plenty of time for doing it. We've only just begun to catch up."

Caleb didn't think he could stand to talk anymore; his head was spinning and he needed to get outside and do something physical. He was also extremely anxious to prove he'd changed from the surly youngster who'd left into a more responsible person.

"There's plenty of time to talk and catch up too," he said, standing up. "Right now we have to make hay while the sun shines. Isn't that the saying?"

Giving everyone his bravest smile, he went outside, and picking up the axe, started splitting logs.

CHAPTER SIXTEEN

Catching Up

By late afternoon, the excitement at his return had died down just a tiny bit, and Caleb had almost exhausted himself chopping and stacking up a huge pile of firewood. Ignoring the pain in his knee, he'd found a rhythm in swinging the axe and lost himself in it. It seemed important to him not to think or feel too much right then; he needed to empty his mind of all thoughts for a while. Otherwise, he'd be completely overwhelmed by what he'd learned and seen in the few hours since his return.

Finally, sweating profusely, Caleb went inside and gulped down several ladles full of cold water from the bucket. Wiping the sweat off his face with his shirt, he announced he'd like to take a catnap before supper. "Just half an hour or so," he told his mother. "I'll wash up before we eat."

"Of course, dear. Just stretch out on my bed for now. We'll fix up something in the loft for you later. I'll wake you when supper's ready."

The moment he lay down, Caleb fell into a profound sleep. Sometime later, an abrupt, raucous squawking broke through his dreams, disturbing his rest. In a groggy and grumpy state, he fought to come to, trying to identify the annoying sound. *It's Jack! The rooster! But it can't be . . . but it is! Holy smokes, the rooster? That means it's morning! Morning?* He squeezed his eyes shut, then opened them again. Jack crowed even louder. Caleb shook his head in disbelief.

Just like the morning he'd woken up in the Whylies' barn, he was startled, with that sense of unfamiliarity, of not knowing where he was for a second. When it came to him that he was in his parents' bed, he couldn't figure out how the sun could be rising and the infernal rooster crowing when in his mind he'd only gone to bed about an hour ago! *I must have slept through dinner and right through the night!* He was amazed.

Caleb's nose twitched as the comforting smell of the morning fire drifted into the bedroom; he could hear his mother stirring in the main room. Swinging his legs over the side of the bed, he sat up, and as he did instinctively every morning, felt the back of his waistband to reassure himself that his treasure was still there. Then he smiled and pulled back the curtain that hung in the doorway instead of a door.

"Good morning, sleepyhead!" His mother was smiling fondly at him. "Guess you really needed that little nap," she teased.

"Sorry, Mother. Seems I was more tired than I thought." He was a bit embarrassed; she was addressing him as she had when he was a little boy, though he didn't resent it as he once might have.

"I guess you were. Don't worry yourself about it. I didn't wake you for supper because I thought you needed your sleep more. There's nothing pressing for you to do today except let me look at that knee. And I do believe those clothes need a thorough washing. You can wear something of your father's while I do that."

At the mention of laundry, Caleb suddenly said, "Oh, that reminds me! I have something for you." And returning to the alcove, he pulled the curtain behind him again, lowered his filthy trousers, and ripped out the sweat-stained sock sewn into the waistband. Two minutes later, he proudly held out the smelly item to his mother, who hesitated to touch it.

"Something for me?" she asked, raising an eyebrow.

"Yes. I know it looks disgusting, but it's really a gift . . . sort of," Caleb said shyly. He watched his mother anxiously as she opened the stinking sock. When she pulled out the bills, her mouth dropped open.

"Caleb! Where did you get this? Oh, dear . . ." She looked questioningly at him.

"I saved it, Mother. From my pay in the mine." He was disappointed that she might think he'd stolen it.

"The mine," she repeated, dumbfounded.

"I haven't had time to tell you anything yet about where I've been, but I got all the way to Sudbury! Worked in a mine for over a year," Caleb said rapidly. "It wasn't much fun underground, and room and board were expensive, but I tried to save every extra penny I could. I thought . . . I thought . . ." Now he didn't know what to say. Mother wasn't as excited as he'd hoped she'd be.

"What did you think, son?"

"I thought it might be almost enough to buy a calf next spring. I guess that sounds kind of stupid now," he mumbled.

Mother wrapped him in her arms; she must have been amazed by how much he'd grown. "Oh, Caleb. You're a good young man, and I'm so proud of you. A calf is a wonderful idea! I was just taken aback for a moment, that's all. Now tell me about the mine. I can't imagine anything as terrible as being underground all day."

As she put water on to boil, they chatted, but despite her questions Caleb wasn't ready to talk about the mine this morning.

"How are Barry and Peter? I was thinking about them on my way home. Do you know how they're doing?"

"Well, Barry's family moved away not long after you left. I think I heard they went to Bracebridge, but I'm not sure. The Boyles would know. They hear all the news at the store."

"Barry's gone?" Caleb said in disbelief. "And you're not sure where?"

"Oh, dear, I am sorry! But I'm fairly certain it is Bracebridge."

Caleb felt disappointed. He'd looked forward to seeing Barry and assumed his friend would still be here. He hesitated a moment before asking, "And Peter?"

"Oh, Peter! He's apprenticing with the blacksmith in Dorset. It's quite a nice opportunity for him. With so many older brothers on the farm, there wasn't much future there for Peter."

Dorset! Bracebridge! Not much chance of ever seeing those two again. It's too far, unless they come home sometime. Everything really has changed.

Before he had a chance to feel too sorry for himself, the girls came down from the loft, their hair all tousled from sleep. They were so happy to see him. This morning they were a bit shy, though, and hung back, just grinning and staring at him as if they couldn't believe he was real.

CHAPTER SEVENTEEN

Bedtime Stories

"What's a mine?" Chantal wanted to know.

When Caleb explained it to her, she said she thought that would be too scary for her.

Every night for the first week of his homecoming, as daylight faded, the family gathered around while Caleb tried to explain what he'd been doing for two years. He realized it was going to take a very long time to relate everything.

Briar wanted to know how far away Sudbury was, and how he got there. Why did he go so far away? That was a difficult question to answer now, and Caleb was glad she hadn't asked the biggest question of all: "Why did you leave in the first place?" He wasn't sure he could put into words the way he'd felt at the time, and he still felt a deep sense of shame that he had abandoned his family when they needed him most.

Samantha wanted to know what kind of people lived in Sudbury. Eskimos? He laughed at that and told her Sudbury was full of people just like themselves, although many were French. They spoke French and had different sounding names.

"Can you speak French?" Briar asked. "Say something in French."

"Probably a lot of the French words I heard in the mine were swear words, and I shouldn't repeat them. But I can count to ten and say good day. 'Good day' is *Bonjour*."

"You can only count to ten? I can count almost to one hundred!" Chantal boasted.

"He means he can count to ten in French," explained Briar. "Do it, Caleb. I've never heard anyone speak French before."

After he did so, Chantal wanted to know how old she was in French. He told her she was still five, but that in French five was *cinq*. For some reason she thought that was hilarious and kept repeating, "Sank, sank, sank. I'm sank years old in French!"

***

Caleb told them about the Laframboise family in whose home he had boarded. Monsieur Laframboise also worked in the mine. Mother wanted to know what her son had been fed, and he told her about delicious tourtière and *tarte au sucre* and other intriguing French-Canadian fare. He didn't tell her those were rare treats, and that most of the time he ate meagre amounts of simple stews and bread. For a growing boy doing hard physical labour, it was often not enough to fill his stomach.

By the end of the week, he'd related most of what he wanted to share. There were other stories he would never tell them: tales of violence in the mine, and bigoted behaviour toward natives and the French. He said nothing of the black-faced, dirt-encrusted men beaten down by life who spent their pay cheques on liquor many weekends, trying to blot from memory the bleakness of their existence while their children went without food.

As he talked, Mother and Samantha would pull out the sewing basket. Something always needed mending or patching. Briar was learning how to darn socks and knit a scarf. Even Chantal had chores. She often peeled potatoes or carrots for the next day, and before they settled in for their chats, she would carry in several armfuls of firewood. At the moment, she was humming and rocking her corn husk doll to sleep.

Sometimes during those evenings, Caleb would suddenly realize he'd put down whatever he was working on and was looking around the sparse cabin and taking in the familiar things of home again. The black cook stove was not just for cooking but also heated the entire cabin. The elegant mahogany table with matching chairs and cabinet, which his parents, perhaps foolishly, had hauled all the way from Toronto, almost filled the space. His sisters' cloaks hung on wall pegs, and nearby sat the two steamer trunks containing his parents' few precious belongings.

It was a typical settlers' cabin with a bedroom for his mother in one corner and a ladder leading to the sleeping loft, where he and his sisters slept on homemade mattresses stuffed with straw. The loft was almost the same size as the main floor, except its walls sloped steeply in, so Caleb could only stand straight up in the very middle, at the roof's highest point.

He watched his mother and sisters, all with their heads bent to their tasks while there was still a bit of light, and thought how hard they worked. There was never a time when anyone could say, "I have nothing to do!" as something always needed doing.

Caleb was busying himself with greasing and sharpening Father's tools, which had been largely unused during the past year. The first task he'd assigned himself was filling in some openings appearing here and there in the chinking between the cabin's log walls. Mosquitoes were sneaking in through those tiny holes and making life miserable, especially at night. But he'd come to realize there were more challenging chores that couldn't be ignored much longer.

His mother was keeping his knee wrapped with cloth she'd torn from an old petticoat, and he'd fashioned a crude sort of crutch from a strong branch. Every night he massaged the knee with horse liniment, and there was some improvement.

When his knee was a bit better, he planned to climb onto the roof and look at the state of the shingles and the chimney. The chimney probably also needed a good cleaning before all the accumulated soot caught fire and burned the house down. Father had always assumed these chores, and now they would be his. Caleb knew he faced enormous responsibilities, but he was determined to do his best.

CHAPTER EIGHTEEN

Big Shoes to Fill

Salty, stinging sweat poured into Caleb's eyes. He rubbed at them with his fist, causing more irritation. *Damn! I can hardly see.* Pulling an old piece of cloth from his back pocket, he roughly wiped his entire face and neck dry. "Time for a break. I'm tired," he grumbled to no one in particular. Laying down the long scythe he'd been swinging to clear the tall grass and weeds, he stretched his aching back and sighed. Today, despite his mother's worries about his sprained knee, he was attempting to clear an area of thick growth so she could enlarge the vegetable garden. However, it was almost impossible to manage the heavy scythe while he still needed to lean on the crutch, and he hadn't accomplished much. He felt discouraged and impatient. *So much needs doing around here! Will we ever catch up?* he wondered.

A bucket of water stayed cool in the shade, and using the tin ladle that sat in it, Caleb scooped up a refreshing mouthful. *Ahh! Heaven!* He smacked his lips and gulped down another mouthful, then splashed some over his face and neck.

Making his way to a stump beside his father's grave, he dropped down on it with a sigh. A wave of sadness washed over him once again as he gazed at the weathered wooden cross inscribed "Jarvis James Lawson." *There were so many things I couldn't wait to tell you!* he thought. *Now, I'll never have that chance, but maybe somehow you know anyway. If you do, I hope you understand.*

Caleb had been lost in thought for just a few minutes when a sudden burst of laughter from Chantal caused him to lift his eyes and smile.

He looked over to watch his sisters playing school. There had been big changes in all three, of course, just as there had been in him. They had certainly grown—that was to be expected. But they had a seriousness he hadn't expected. He knew it was the result of their father's death and the hard times that followed. That's why Chantal's laughter was so reassuring to hear.

The impact of his father's death was fresher for him. He had only been home for two weeks and was still finding the dreadful loss difficult to believe, but the longer he was home, the more he noticed how poor his family's situation really was. He realized he was going to have to start working for Mr. Whylie as soon as possible.

He looked down at father's shoes on his feet. They were a symbol of what lay ahead. He had decided to try to fill his father's shoes and become the breadwinner.

Splash! Caleb recognized the wet sound of dirty wash water being tossed from the laundry tub on the far side of the cabin, followed by happy humming as his mother appeared, carrying a soggy bundle of dripping clothes. She stopped and took in the scene. Caleb, seeing her happy face, could almost read her mind: *"All my children together at last!"*

He thought, *She's pleased, but she can read my mind. She's worried something will happen and I'll leave again.*

In some ways, leaving would be easier than staying. Ever since he'd heard about his old friend Peter apprenticing with the blacksmith in Dorset, he kept thinking how much that appealed to him as well. A "smithy" did useful work, producing and repairing tools and other items people needed. Farming was definitely useful; after all, it fed his family, but his father had not had much luck with it, and Caleb didn't believe he could do much better.

But he knew it was useless to dream of becoming a smithy; he'd made his decision. Watching his sisters, he noticed how relieved they were to have him home, and that made him feel better. At least he'd been able to remove one worry from their lives. Goodness knows many others remained.

His reverie was broken by Chantal's happy shout upon spying their mother. "Mama, I can count to one hundred and twenty-five! Do you want to hear me? Do you?" She was so excited, she was dancing with delight.

Mother smiled. "Of course I do, dear. But first let me hang up these wet clothes."

CHAPTER NINETEEN

Samantha's Dilemma

Samantha had watched her brother as he tried to swing the heavy scythe and could see how he struggled. Now he sat beside Father's grave, lost in thought and looking sad. She worried about him, and not just because of his sore knee. Obviously, Caleb felt he should assume his father's role in supporting the family, and she wondered if he could. She had always helped Mother as much as possible, but she was only eleven and a girl. She realized she could help Caleb clear the field and plant it, and she would, but there were still other jobs most people thought only a young man could do. She couldn't work in the lumber camps, of course, unless as a cook, and even then she'd have to be older. Mother likely wouldn't ever let her go there anyway. She couldn't wait to be older, but she also couldn't wait for the school to reopen. If only a teacher could be found somewhere!

Samantha shared her mother's dream for her to become a teacher. It was the only dream she allowed herself, yet it seemed an impossible one. *Even if Father were still alive, how could I learn to be a teacher when I can't even go to school? And even if I could go to school, mother couldn't afford to send me to a teacher's college. Sometimes there are scholarships for top students, but how can I be a top student without going to school? It's like going around in circles, and it all comes back to the same thing . . . no teacher!*

"You're not paying attention, Samantha!" Briar scolded.

"Listen to me count!" Chantal cried.

Samantha sighed; she just wasn't in the mood for playing school today, but her sisters were enjoying themselves. Briar liked being the pretend teacher, and Samantha knew she longed to go back to school too. Briar also worried tremendously about their mother and watched her like a hawk. Having already lost her father, she was terrified of losing her remaining parent.

"What will happen to us if we become orphans?" she had asked her big sister more than once.

Samantha believed this worry had caused Briar's bad dreams ever since Father died, and clearly it was a huge relief to have their big brother home. Poor Briar was reluctant to let him out of her sight; she had sheepishly told Samantha that every morning when she woke up, she checked to see that he was really still there! Samantha understood this. She felt the same sense of relief at her brother's return. Even so, a part of her still worried he might feel overwhelmed by his new responsibilities and leave again.

Reluctantly, she turned her attention back to the game of school just as her mother returned to the clearing with her bundle of wet laundry. As she paused to take in the scene of all her children together, a smile lit up her face, and that, in turn, made Samantha smile. *Maybe it will all work out after all,* she thought.

CHAPTER TWENTY

The Stranger Returns

On a sweltering afternoon a few days later, Caleb dipped a wooden
stick into the bucket of mortar he'd mixed and carried on repairing the holes
in the chinking between the log walls. Although he tried to work in the shade,
the sun caught up with him as he progressed around the cabin, and he was hot
and thirsty but determined to get the job done. Everyone was fed up with the
mosquitoes and blackflies getting in the cabin through the gaps and feasting
on them. At least the mosquitoes feasted; folks claimed blackflies didn't bite
indoors. Whether they did or they didn't, they were equally annoying.

He heard Chantal coming out of the cabin and calling him. "Caleb,
I need—" she started to say, then screamed, "Indians!" at the top of her lungs.
The terror in her voice caused Caleb to drop his bucket and brush, and their

mother to come tearing out of the cabin.

Chantal stood rooted to the ground, pointing a trembling finger at a man and a boy standing in the forest, as still as the ancient trees around them. Caleb grabbed Chantal and picked her up. She was trembling at the unexpected sight of these strangers. Out of the corner of his eye, he could see Samantha and Briar huddled in the doorway. Chantal's scream must have alarmed them.

"Sh-h-h," he murmured. "Don't be scared."

All the time he was wondering who the strangers were and why they were just standing there in the trees.

The man touched the boy on the shoulder, and the two slowly moved out of the woods toward them but stopped some distance away. . Caleb realized they were native people. Each was dressed in a plaid shirt and work pants, but instead of wearing heavy boots they moved silently in traditional moccasins. *That's why I didn't hear them approaching,* he thought.

The man looked nervously at Caleb and his mother. He pointed to a pole he carried, which was stacked with fish, and then pointed to Caleb. He held the fish in front of him, as if offering them, and nodded. Without talking, he seemed to be saying, "These are for you." Caleb didn't know what to think. Like Chantal, he was a bit unsettled by the sudden appearance of strangers out of the woods.

Oh, boy! What does this mean? What should I do? If Father were here, he'd know.

Suddenly, he heard his mother say, "The rabbits. It's the rabbit man! I recognize him now."

She gave Chantal a reassuring pat on the shoulder and then walked toward the man, ready to accept the fish, and said, "Thank you. Thank you for the rabbits, and thank you for these. We are very grateful, but why have you brought them? What is your name?"

"I am Tom Big Canoe." Indicating the boy beside him, he said, "Jonah Big Canoe, my son." The boy appeared to be about ten or eleven, and his big eyes looked uncertain.

Mother gave him a big smile and said, "Thank you, Jonah. These are beautiful fish. Did you catch some of them?" This brought a shy nod from the boy.

Caleb's heart was slowing down a bit, but he was still unsure of the situation. Mother, however, seemed quite calm.

"I am Beatrice Lawson," she said to the man. "This is my son and my daughters."

Tom Big Canoe nodded. "Your man, Jarvis Lawson, helped me near lumber camp last year. Big pine fell, pinned me down. Jarvis Lawson saved my life. I come before, bring rabbits, see you alone. Your boy was not here. I think maybe your man away. Then I see grave. Jarvis Lawson was good man."

My father saved this man's life! Caleb felt a rush of pride. He watched his mother's eyes fill with tears.

She spoke softly. "Yes, he was a very good man. Thank you. I didn't know he helped you. He never spoke of it. But he wouldn't have—he was also a very modest man. I wish he were here to receive your gifts, Mr. Big Canoe . . . and Jonah. He would have been so pleased to see you again, I'm sure."

A few moments of awkward silence followed while she collected herself. Caleb put his arm around Chantal, and the two older girls slowly came out of the cabin, still holding on to each other. Then, to his complete astonishment, his mother exclaimed, "Oh, where are my manners? You must stay and eat with us. We'll clean the fish and put them on the fire right away. They'll be delicious. You must stay. We so seldom have guests." Caleb heard Samantha gasp.

Mother seemed to have embarrassed Tom with her sudden gush of enthusiasm. He looked down at the ground and mumbled that he and Jonah could not stay, but that they would come again one day. Mother appeared reluctant to let them go, and Jonah looked as if he might want to stay, but both accepted Tom's decision.

"Do you live nearby, Mr. Big Canoe? I mean, does your family have a camp nearby or are you just passing through?"

"We come with Chief Big Wind. Our people hunt, fish the big lake."

Mother said she and her family would be glad to see him, and indeed his whole family, if they'd come, any time at all. Then they all watched as the two Indians turned and walked back into the forest, turning just once to raise a hand, as if in a salute, before vanishing from sight.

Holding the long pole crammed with speckled trout, Mother turned to survey her children. All four stood quietly watching the forest where Tom and Jonah had disappeared so completely. With a catch in her voice she said, "Mr. Big Canoe is right. Your father was a very good man, a wonderful man, and I really miss him. He would have been pleased to know that his good deed was so appreciated. I hope you will always remember what a good man he was and try your best to follow his example."

They all nodded sombrely. Caleb began to think about the encounter. It had been a pleasant one, but still they'd been taken by surprise, and he couldn't help but wonder whether or not he would be able to protect his family if strangers intent on harm appeared. He felt overwhelmed by such responsibility.

As if sensing the need to lighten the moment, Mother smiled and said, "Now, let's clean these fish! We're going to enjoy a feast tonight."

CHAPTER TWENTY-ONE

A Turn for the Better

A week later, Caleb walked to the Whylie farm and told Mr. Whylie he was ready to start working. The farmer, a man of few words, nodded and showed him where he kept his tools. The agreement was that Caleb would spend two to three days a week there and go home for the rest of the week. As well as his small salary, he'd get his meals and could sleep in the small loft in the house.

Three weeks had passed, with Caleb helping Mr. Whylie repair the barn and the roof of the house. He'd learned that in another month or so, many neighbours would arrive to help harvest the Whylies' wheat crop. He had always looked forward to harvesting bees; a day of hard labour was always accompanied by plentiful, hearty food and ended with a party. Someone was sure to produce a fiddle, and even the most exhausted worker would rise to the tune, choose a partner, and dance.

Today he and Mr. Whylie were in the pasture beside the house, pulling out small tree stumps with the help of a strong draught horse the farmer had borrowed from his neighbour. It was difficult and strenuous work for man and horse, but Caleb wasn't about to complain. He'd experienced working in the depths of a dark, dank mine, and he much preferred being out in the sunshine, even on a sweltering August day like today.

He had decided that Mr. Whylie was a conundrum, a puzzle. On the first day they'd met, he'd held a gun on him. The next day, he'd offered him a job! He was gentle and kind with Mrs. Whylie and May but usually very gruff with Caleb. So far, he'd only needed Caleb for two days a week, which was fine because it gave Caleb time to help his mother out during the other days. All the same, he was hoping Mr. Whylie would soon ask him to come at least three days a week. *I could sure use the money—that's for sure*, he thought. He wanted to buy that calf, and he'd nearly saved the amount needed. When the calf became fully grown, his family would be able to add milk, cream, and perhaps even some cheese to their diet, each of which would be a delicious addition.

Mrs. Whylie struggled across the field with a heavy bucket of cold water and a tin cup. As they paused for the welcome, refreshing drink and a few moments' rest, there wasn't much conversation. "I'd like to pay your mother a visit one of these days, if you think she wouldn't mind," Mrs. Whylie said as though she'd just had the idea.

"Oh, I'm sure she'd really like that, Mrs. Whylie," Caleb replied. "Not too many people come out our way. We're so far from the village."

"Good. Please tell her when you go home this week that I'll stop by in three or four days."

"Yes, ma'am. I expect she'll be pleased." As he was speaking to her, he looked past her shoulder and noticed some dust rising in the distance. "Looks like someone is coming along the road," Caleb said, and the Whylies both turned to look in the direction he was indicating.

Charlie seemed to materialize out of nowhere, and agitatedly began barking, running back and forth along the edge of the field.

"Quiet, Charlie!" Mrs. Whylie admonished. "Someone's coming. Yes, we know. We see him." Charlie continued his barking, but a little less ferociously. "Hush, Charlie! Sit!" Mrs. Whylie wagged a finger at the dog, who finally sat down but started to whine.

The Whylies and Caleb watched as a horse and rider materialized, approaching at a sedate trot. A tall man sat straight in the saddle. His dark horse was laden with heavy saddlebags placed behind the rider, who slowed the horse to a walk and finally a halt before them.

"Good morning," the stranger said and courteously tipped his hat to Mrs. Whylie. Charlie issued a low warning growl.

"Mornin'," Jim Whylie responded, and Caleb followed suit. "Help ya?" Mr. Whylie said tersely.

"Yes, I hope so," the fellow said. He dismounted and removed the bit so his horse could nibble at the weeds and bits of grass beside the road. Caleb judged him to be about the same age his own father would have been and very fit but taller. "I came to introduce myself," the man said with a friendly smile. "I'm Dr. Paul. My daughter Heather and I have just moved to town. She's been hired as the new schoolmistress."

"Oh, my gracious! A new schoolmistress. That's wonderful news!" exclaimed Mrs. Whylie. "Our Elsie May will be so thrilled to return to school. So will all the children—and their parents! It's been so long, we'd about given up hope of a new teacher ever coming here. And you say you're a doctor?"

Before Dr. Paul could answer, Mr. Whylie interrupted his wife to say, "We're the Whylies. Pleased to meet ya." He and the doctor shook hands. Then remembering Caleb, he added, "This here is Caleb Lawson," and nodded in Caleb's general direction. Caleb and the doctor also shook hands. "You planning on doin' some doctorin' here?"

"I sure do," answered Dr. Paul. "There's just the two of us, so when my daughter was hired to teach here, I decided to pull up stakes and come with her. Make a fresh start."

Caleb happened to glance at the Whylies as the doctor said this last part; both of them wore puzzled expressions, as if neither had understood what their visitor had just said. Caleb thought he understood why; after all, it was unusual for an established doctor to talk about pulling up stakes and making a fresh start, and the idea of a man following his daughter to her new job was even more so. Most unusual of all was that a doctor's daughter would even want or need a job.

Caleb glanced back at the doctor. Perhaps the man had also noticed the look on the Whylies' faces. "My wife passed away a couple of years ago," he said by way of explanation. "This move will be good for both of us."

"I'm sorry for your loss," Mrs. Whylie said with sincerity. "Where have you moved from?"

"Originally from a small village this side of Niagara Falls. Used to be called Newark; now it's Niagara-on-the-Lake. But the past couple of years, we were in Toronto, where my daughter was receiving her teacher's training."

"You've come an awful long way," Mr. Whylie remarked.

"That we have, but I think we're going to like it here. At any rate, I decided to ride out to a few farms and let people know that school will be starting up again the first Monday in September. You could help us by letting others know. I'm sure I'll miss some families."

Turning to Caleb, he inquired, "What about you, young man? Will you be coming to school, or are you finished with that?"

"Don't expect so, sir." Caleb was embarrassed. "Haven't been to school for a long time, but I've got three sisters who'll be glad to hear it'll be open again."

"Well, you tell your parents about it. I hope you and your sisters will all be able to attend. Guess it's time I headed home now. Armon here has had quite a workout this morning, haven't you, boy?" he said to his grazing horse. At the sound of his name, the animal looked up and whinnied. The doctor whistled, and Armon obediently trotted over and stood still while his master put the bit back on and picked up the reins. Hoisting himself back into the saddle, Dr. Paul waved a cheerful goodbye.

The three watched him turn Armon around and head toward the village. Charlie gave a yip and ran after them for a short distance but soon gave up and ambled back, nose to the ground, sniffing Armon's scent.

"Well, will wonders never cease? A new schoolmistress and a doctor, too!" exclaimed Mrs. Whylie. "Can't remember the last time there was a doctor around here. Maybe he'll be able to do something for our Andrew."

Mr. Whylie merely grunted and told Caleb they had no more time to waste and should get back to pulling up some stumps.

CHAPTER TWENTY-TWO

Good News

Two days later, as Caleb approached his own home, a sweet and enticing aroma wafted toward him, and immediately his mouth watered in anticipation; Mother and the girls must be making jam.

They'd picked lots of wild raspberries and blackberries; it took plenty just to make one jar of jam. They'd all be picking every day now until berry season was past, competing with the bears for whatever fruit there was. However, in the middle of winter, when they could slather the sweet spread on warm slices of bread fresh from the oven, they'd be so grateful. Caleb's mouth watered at the very thought.

Sitting down at the table, he thought once again how glad he was that he'd returned to his family. "Mrs. Whylie has a few apple trees. She said she'd give us at least a bushel when they're ready in a month or so."

"Well, we'd certainly appreciate that, wouldn't we, girls?" said his mother. "Nice fresh apples—we could put up some applesauce or apple butter."

"And maybe an apple pie?" suggested Caleb.

"And maybe an apple pie," repeated Mother with a little smile. "Oh, and she said she'd like to come by for a visit in a day or so. I told her you'd surely enjoy that. I hope that's all right."

"Of course, son. I'll look forward to her visit. Thank you."

"How's May?" asked Samantha. "I wish I could see her now and then. I miss my school friends."

"Well, I have some other news that'll make you happy. And you too, Mother. There's a new teacher, and school's going to start again the first Monday in September!"

"Really?" This came from Mother, Samantha, and Briar almost in unison. The excitement lit up their faces.

"How do you know?" asked Briar.

"The Whylies had a visitor two days ago. He's the new teacher's father, and he was visiting some families in the area to let them know that school will be starting again. His name is Dr. Paul. They just moved into the village."

"Dr. Paul?" asked Mother. "A doctor? Will he set up a practice here? It's a long time since any of us has seen a doctor. Isn't that something, now? A doctor in the village!" She sat down to ponder this amazing news. Not only a new teacher, which was wonderful enough, but possibly a doctor, too!

"He said he's going to see patients," Caleb answered. "I don't think I've ever been to a doctor, have I?"

"Just a couple of times when you were a baby. You and Samantha," his mother replied. "That was before we came to Muskoka. And there was one doctor in the area then that I know of, but he eventually died. A new doctor will be great news for all the families around here."

At dinnertime, all the conversation revolved around the return to school.

"Will I have a real desk?" Chantal asked. "Is it a long walk? Will we take our lunch to school? Will there be other little girls to play with?"

"Slow down, dear. One question at a time!" Mother said, laughing.

"I'm so excited!" Briar exclaimed. "But it's a long walk every day. How will we get there? Especially in the winter? We've waited so long for a teacher, it would be sad if we had to miss a lot of school."

"We'll work something out," their mother replied. "Without your father here to take you in the wagon, it won't be easy, but we'll do it. For now, you can walk. When winter comes, we'll see."

"It's too bad the wagon is in such a sad state," Caleb said. "And old Bonnie isn't up to the job anymore either."

"Are you going to come to school with us, Caleb?" Samantha asked.

"I don't think so. I've been away from school for too long."

Caleb looked at his mother, who didn't say anything. He knew she longed for him get an education, but she also acknowledged the stark reality that his work for the Whylies was providing badly needed income for the family. It was a difficult dilemma. He had enjoyed school, but he had been away from it now for two years and felt that, at fifteen, his school days were truly over. He could read and write well enough, and he was very quick with mathematics. That would likely be all he needed if he was going to spend his life farming, hunting, and fishing.

That evening, as they all sat chatting, Caleb related what he'd been doing at the Whylie farm the last few days and answered Samantha's questions about her friend, May.

"What about that nice young man, Andrew Whylie?" his mother asked. "Do you ever see him? I wonder how often he's able to visit his family?"

Caleb wondered how Mother could think Andrew Whylie was a "nice young man." "No, I haven't seen him since that first day I met all the Whylies."

"And how about the rest of the family? What are they like?"

"Mrs. Whylie is very nice, and May is fine, I guess," Caleb said. "But Mr. Whylie is kind of gruff."

"Well, it takes all kinds. The main thing is, he seems to be honest and treating you well. Perhaps in time you'll find him easier."

"I hope so."

"What's gruff?" asked Chantal. "Is he like *Three Billy Goats Gruff* in the story?"

"Well," Caleb told her with a big twinkle in his eye, "you might say he's a bit of an old goat!"

"Caleb! You know better than to talk like that!" Mother chided.

"Sorry, Mother, but he really is! Either an old goat or an old bear."

"Don't talk about bears!" cried Chantal. "I don't want to see any more bears!"

CHAPTER TWENTY-THREE

Thief!

Caleb entered the general store whistling and smiling. It was the kind of cloudless, blue-sky summer day that lifted the spirits, and he felt cheerful.

"Good morning, Mrs. Boyle."

"Morning, Caleb. Are you on your own today?"

"Yes, ma'am. Mr. Whylie sent me in for some things."

"How's your mother keeping?"

"She's fine, thank you, ma'am."

"Glad to hear it. What can we do for you?"

"Mr. Whylie needs some four-inch nails, a small case of them, if you have some."

"Over here, Caleb." Mr. Boyle was standing near some shelves halfway down the store where several types of nails, hammers, axes, knives, and other hardware items were stored. Large crates of other goods stood on the floor, and Caleb had to slide in among them to reach him.

"Four-inch nails, was it?" Mr Boyle asked.

"Yes, sir." Looking at the merchandise, Caleb's eye immediately homed in on one particular knife. *Boy, that's a beauty!* He picked it up, admiring an intricately carved pattern on its handle and running his finger along it. *This'd be great for hunting and fishing and all kinds of things.* He hefted its weight and it felt good—until he looked at the price tag. *Impossible!* He put it down again.

"Nice knife, isn't it? Bet you could use one like that."

"Oh, yes, sir. I sure could. It's a great knife, but I couldn't afford it right now. Maybe someday, though."

Mr. Boyle had finished searching the shelves. "Haven't got what you want up here. I'll ask Andrew to get some from the back room." As the storekeeper moved to the rear of the store, Caleb picked the knife up again, turning it over and over in his hand, getting a feel for it. Andrew Whylie appeared with the case of nails. He frowned as he handed it over to Caleb without saying a word. *Nice to see you, too!* Caleb wanted to laugh. Then he laid the knife down once again with a regretful glance.

"Is there anything else you need, Caleb?" Mr. Boyle asked as the two walked to the front of the store.

At the cash register, Mrs. Boyle said, "Oh, I almost forgot! There's a letter for your mother." She reached behind her and took an envelope from the wooden slots where both outgoing and incoming mail were kept.

"A letter?" Taking the envelope, he read the return address. *Alberta! Uncle Wesley's in Alberta.* He knew how pleased his mother would be to hear from her brother and couldn't wait to bring it to her. Letters were rare, and this one would be a welcome surprise.

"Thanks, Mrs. Boyle. I'll be seeing her tomorrow."

"I hope it's good news!"

"I hope so too!" *But what if it isn't? Maybe something's wrong with Uncle Wesley.* He decided not to borrow trouble and put that thought out of his mind. "Well, goodbye!"

"Goodbye, Caleb. Say hello to your mother for me."

"Yes, ma'am."

He hefted the case of nails onto his shoulder, tucked the mysterious letter into his back pocket, and whistling again, headed back to the Whylie farm.

***

With a sly smile, Andrew watched him leave, then moved back to stacking shelves, and the Boyles returned to their various tasks. No more customers came in for the rest of the morning. All the while, Andrew's prying eyes watched the Boyles and he listened to their occasional conversations, waiting to set his scheme in motion.

It was after lunch when Mr. Boyle started muttering to himself as he searched some shelves.

"What on earth are you mumbling about?" his wife demanded.

"That knife. It was here a little while ago, but now I can't find it."

"Some days you wouldn't be able to find your own head if it weren't screwed on!" his wife retorted. "Where did you last see it?"

"Right here. Young Caleb was looking at it. I thought he might have bought it. He sure liked the looks of it."

The two looked at each other a minute. "You don't think . . . ?" Mr. Boyle looked at his wife.

"Never!" she replied.

"Well, no one else has been in."

"Just keep looking for it! It'll turn up."

Muttering even more darkly, Mr. Boyle set about moving crates and other items in his search, which proved fruitless.

"Andrew!" he shouted. "Have you seen that knife with the fancy hilt?"

"No, sir. Last I saw of it, Caleb had it in his hand. Haven't seen it since."

"Well, keep a sharp eye out for it."

***

Late in the afternoon, a discouraged Mr. Boyle told his wife, "It's the only explanation. I've turned this place upside down, and there's no knife! That young fellow must've pocketed it."

"Lower your voice, Cyril!" Mrs. Boyle whispered, looking to where two ladies were examining some bolts of cloth. "It's a fairly big knife. It wouldn't be that easy to walk out with."

"And not that hard either, if a fellow really coveted it." Mr. Boyle was now whispering too.

"Well, we can't accuse him of it without proof, and we haven't any. There's nothing to be done about it. With luck it'll still turn up."

"Bah! It's gone for good, and that young fellow took it!"

Andrew, hovering nearby, had overheard just enough to know his plan was working at last. *Time to add the finishing touch. This'll teach you, Caleb! Things aren't going to be as easy around here as you seem to think.*

He stepped forward. "Excuse me, Mr. Boyle, but I couldn't help overhearing, and there's something I should perhaps tell you."

"Well, what is it?" Mr. Boyle snapped.

Briefly, Andrew hesitated as he began having second thoughts about what he was about to do. Then he pictured Caleb working on the farm with his father. He still couldn't believe his father had hired the runaway. *It should be me!* He seethed inwardly. *I'm the one belongs on the farm, working with my father, not that kid. If it wasn't for that damn accident, I would be.*

"Spit it out, boy!"

Andrew swallowed hard, and then the fatal words tumbled out. "Yes, sir. I know you don't like gossip, but, well, I did hear something troubling recently . . . about Caleb Lawson."

CHAPTER TWENTY-FOUR

A Letter from Afar

Medicine Hat, Alberta,

March 1, 1879

My dearest sister,

It is with great sadness that I write. Only this week did news reach me of your dear husband's untimely passing. The postal service has not served us well; the letter informing me of his death must have gone far astray, as I see by the date that it arrived over one year late. How I wish I had been closer to you in your time of sorrow, Beatrice.

Jarvis was a true gentleman, and one held in the highest regard by all who knew him. I am proud to have called him a friend and pleased that it was I who introduced you to each other. My prayers are with you, my dear sister, and with my nieces and nephew. I imagine that Caleb is now old enough to be a great help to you. If he is anything like his father, he will be a reliable and dependable young man. Samantha, Briar, and Chantal must be growing up quickly too, and I am sure they are a comfort to you.

I think of you often and wonder how you are faring in Muskoka. Will you stay, now that you are without your Jarvis? Should you return to Toronto, please write and inform me of your address. If you would consider joining me here, it would please me greatly to welcome you and help you settle. Please do not dismiss this idea out of hand, dear sister. Give it serious consideration. Alberta is an exciting place, and I believe you would like it very much.

Despite a difficult start, I now have a small cattle ranch near Medicine Hat. This is a life I could never have imagined, growing up in Toronto. I imagine you feel the same about Muskoka. I have not married but am presently courting a most charming and lovely lady, Miss Leah Probert, the daughter of a neighbouring rancher. As she appears to enjoy my company as much as I enjoy hers, I hope to have good news for you before long.

Beatrice, you should receive a letter before long from my solicitors, Messrs. Anderson and Russell in Toronto. I pray that this letter to you, and my instructions to them, do not take as long to arrive as your letter to me. They are to forward a small sum on my behalf, which I sincerely hope will be of benefit to you and the children at this time. It is the least I can do. If you have any need of further assistance, you have only to let me know, either directly or through my solicitors.

Once again, dear sister, I send my deepest condolences on your great loss. Please write again, that I may know how you and my dear nieces and nephew are faring.

I remain your loving brother,

— Wesley

The children gathered around to hear their mother read the letter. She first read it to herself. As they watched, they saw a falling tear, then a smile, and finally, a surprised look.

"Oh, my goodness!"

"What is it? What is it?" Samantha cried.

"Is it good news?" Caleb asked.

"Yes, indeed. It's always good news to hear from your Uncle Wesley. I'll read it to you now, but no questions till I've finished, promise?"

After receiving their promises, Mother read the letter aloud. She was just as emotional reading it the second time as she had been the first.

"Uncle Wesley's getting married!" Samantha was excited.

"I wonder what the small sum is, and when we'll hear from his solicitors?" Caleb asked, thinking of more practical matters. "That's awfully kind of him."

"It is kind. Whatever the amount, it will certainly be most welcome. I can't believe it took that long for my letter to reach him. I couldn't understand why I hadn't heard from him in all this time and worried something might have happened to him. What a relief to know he's well and may even marry. Isn't that wonderful?"

"Medicine Hat is a funny name for a place," Briar said.

"It does seem unusual, doesn't it?" Mother agreed. "There's probably an interesting story behind that. Why don't you ask Miss Paul? I'm sure she can help you find it on the map too."

Mother read the letter to herself once again.

"Oh, it's so marvellous to have heard from Wesley! Just knowing he's well has made me very happy."

"Yes, it's good news all around, I'd say," said Caleb with a happy grin. He could tell this letter from his uncle had gone a long way toward lifting his mother's spirits, and he felt a slight easing of his own worries too. No matter what amount of money came their way, it would be an enormous help.

CHAPTER TWENTY-FIVE

Andrew's Nightmare

From behind the stacked flour barrels, Andrew Whylie watched Caleb's mother talking to the Boyles. Mrs. Boyle was buying some of the woman's eggs to sell in the store. Mr. Boyle, as usual, was sitting on a stool, letting his wife do most of the work. However, Andrew noticed that both were being a little less friendly toward Mrs. Lawson. He wondered if she had noticed as well.

Normally, Andrew would have no reason to take any particular interest in the Lawson family, but now that their missing boy was back, all that had changed, and Andrew was not happy. That Caleb was working on his family's farm was causing him distress.

Andrew loved that farm with every fibre of his being; it was as if its pure streams ran in his veins instead of blood. Almost since he learned to walk and explore the fields, he had dreamed of the day when he would work them alongside his father. He knew that, in time, the farm would be handed over to him to run.

After all, he thought. *I'm the only son; it's supposed to be mine one day!*

He was angry, and he could admit to himself that he was also jealous: angry because the accident at the lumber camp had ruined both his back and his life, and jealous because young Caleb Lawson was taking the place that was rightfully his. *Well,* he swore to himself, *I'll see that it doesn't last.*

The day that expensive knife had mysteriously "disappeared" from the store, Andrew had set the wheels in motion to get rid of Caleb by inventing a rumour that the boy had spent time in jail. *That little tale should reach Father's ears soon,* he thought. But he was frustrated by Mr. Boyle's lack of action. *What's the matter with him? Why hasn't he confronted Caleb about stealing that knife?*

On his worst days, Andrew moved with considerable pain. When he was tired, he would find himself limping too. He was only nineteen but felt like a very old man. Every twinge and spasm reminded him of that desperate moment a little over a year ago when he found himself unable to escape an enormous rolling log. He couldn't even escape the terror in his sleep; it haunted his dreams.

Even now his mind betrayed him, dragging him back to the scene at the logging camp, with the horrifying images and deafening sounds of that late winter day. Once again, he watched as the crew manoeuvred a final massive log atop an already looming pile.

Men shouted instructions to each other and swore in English and French: "Move it!" "Let 'er roll!" "Bloody hell!" Enormous logs thundered and crashed into place. The noise was ear-splitting, but the men worked with a practiced ease Andrew admired; they had all performed this task a hundred times before.

Everything appeared stable, and Andrew had just turned to walk away when one errant log slipped the tiniest fraction of an inch, emitting a low grinding and groaning sound that alerted those closest to it. As it loosened and started to roll, the men's shouts became frantic. Andrew whirled around, and the sight of that monstrous log crashing toward him struck sheer terror in his heart. Briefly, he stood transfixed, unable to move.

"Run!" the men screamed, breaking his trance. Like a jackrabbit, he sprang up, then slipped on a treacherous patch of black ice and went down with a heavy thud.

Now he closed his eyes, as if by doing so he could block out the vivid memories. *I didn't stand a cha*nce, he thought. His ears still rang with the terrified shouts of his crew and the earth-shaking rumble of that runaway log. Thank goodness the men managed to hold the others in place, or the tragedy would have been much greater.

The blow had knocked him out, and when he came to the sharp intensity of the pain nearly caused him to pass out again. Opening his eyes, he focused on the slightly blurry but decidedly anxious face of the camp's doc hovering over him. He knew by the man's sober expression that his injuries were serious. "Sober" was not a word normally used to describe the doc. All liquor was forbidden in the camp, but the men figured the doc must have had a secret supply.

After two days of bed rest and strong doses of laudanum for pain, Andrew was bundled with great care onto the back of a sleigh to be transported home. Men with solemn faces gathered round to say goodbye, each raising an arm in a sombre salute as the sleigh moved off. Andrew's drugged mind managed to form a coherent thought before he drifted off to sleep. *Every one of them is probably thinking, "Thank God it's not me!"*

His body took such a jostling on that journey that he would have passed out again from the pain if not for the extra laudanum the doc had insisted he take. He was relieved it also caused him to sleep through most of the trip. When Andrew caught a glimpse of the horrified looks his parents immediately hid behind their stiff, overly bright smiles, he wished he had died under that log.

After his long and slow recovery, the Boyles had offered Andrew work, but he didn't know how long that would last. He wasn't able to lift anything heavy, but he was good at organizing and stocking shelves and helping to keep the account books straight. He wasn't fond of working inside; he preferred the outdoors, but now he had no choice. He felt trapped, and some days, when the pain was particularly severe, his thoughts would darken again, and the morbid thought returned: *Would have been better if the damned thing had killed me!*

Damn! Mrs. Lawson was now coming toward him. He didn't want to talk to her. She always said hello and chatted with him for a few minutes. He didn't know why, but she seemed to enjoy talking to him. He was always polite to her in return. *Mother would be proud,* he thought with wicked sarcasm. *At least some of her attempts to teach me manners must have worked.*

"Good morning, Andrew. How are you?"

"Morning, Mrs. Lawson. I'm doing just fine."

"I'm glad to hear it. I had a lovely visit from your mother the other day. It was kind of her to take the time. I really enjoyed her company."

"That's nice."

"Yes, and I can't tell you how thankful I am that your father has given my Caleb some work. It helps us make ends meet a little better."

Andrew just nodded.

"Have you met Caleb? I know there's a difference in your ages, but I thought you two might become friends. Most of his old school pals have moved away."

"Yes, we've met a couple of times."

"I'm glad. Maybe you'll see more of each other. Well, I must be off. It's been lovely seeing you again, Andrew."

"Goodbye, Mrs. Lawson." He managed a smile. *That'll be the day when I become friends with Caleb Lawson!* he thought.

It was strange, but after she left, he was more depressed than ever. She was a kind lady, and he meant her no harm. It was her son he couldn't stand. *Don't let it get to you,* he thought.

CHAPTER TWENTY-SIX

Meeting
Miss Heather

The next day was Saturday, and Andrew was still in a foul mood, feeling sorry for himself, when Miss Heather Paul entered the store. Andrew had seen the young teacher three or four times before, and each time she took his breath away. He found it hard not to stare. She was so lively and lovely that he was thoroughly entranced. But before she could look his way and perhaps speak to him, he slipped into the storeroom and waited for her to finish her shopping and leave.

His escape didn't last long, however, as he heard Mr. Boyle bellow, "Andrew! Fetch that new bolt of cloth that just arrived the other day and bring it here." He was trapped. There was nothing to do but fetch the cloth.

Andrew limped to the counter and laid the bolt of flower-patterned fabric down. As he did, the sweet floral scent of the young woman's perfume surrounded him. He'd never known anything like it. Suddenly, he realized he'd stood there, mesmerized, a moment too long and felt embarrassed.

"Good afternoon, Miss Paul." He blushed and turned to leave, but it wasn't going to be that easy.

"Good afternoon, Mr. Whylie," she replied with a smile that could melt icebergs. "I believe I have the pleasure of teaching your sister, May. I didn't realize the connection until she spoke of her big brother recently."

"Oh, yes . . . May. How is she doing in school? I'm afraid I haven't been home for a while. I live here, you know. I have a room." *Why are you telling her all this? She doesn't care where you live. Smarten up! You're babbling like a fool.*

"Yes, I know. May's doing just fine. She's a lovely girl, but I gather she's somewhat lonely now that she's the only one at home. I think she'd love to see you."

"Well, I'll see what I can do. It's rather difficult . . ." Automatically, Andrew gazed down at his bad leg.

He could feel his face turning even redder and was horrified that the lovely young woman had noticed. Now, from the flush of colour in her cheeks, it appeared she was also embarrassed. *What a mess!* he thought. He was about to excuse himself and go back to the storeroom when she spoke again, all in a rush to cover up the awkward moment.

"How thoughtless of me! Of course, there mustn't be many opportunities for you to hitch a ride with someone headed in that direction on your day off. Well, perhaps one day May might come to town herself to see you."

"Well, now that my father has a new wagon, he can come for me a little more often." Andrew began to mumble in a futile attempt to ease her discomfort.

She remained flustered, her lovely eyes darting around the store. Turning to Mrs. Boyle, she said, "This is a beautiful piece of cloth indeed. Wouldn't it sew up nicely into a blouse?"

Andrew made his escape and returned to stacking canned goods on a shelf. He tried not to think about Miss Paul, but that was impossible. It was maddening because if he were his old self, fit and healthy, he would look forward to seeing her more, maybe even invite her to a dance or take her for a buggy ride, but all that was nothing but a hopeless dream now. He certainly couldn't dance, and what young woman would want to take a chance on someone as damaged as he was? A beautiful girl like Heather Paul would have her pick of healthy young men.

"Well, good day." He heard the teacher concluding her transaction with Mrs. Boyle. *Good. She's leaving! What a relief.* But to his horror, instead of leaving she turned around and walked toward him again.

"Mr. Whylie, it occurred to me that perhaps my father and I could drive May into town after school one day, and the two of you could have a little visit."

"That's very kind, but it's too much trouble for you and Dr. Paul."

"Oh, not at all. It would give May great pleasure, I know, and it's a simple thing for us to do. Would it be all right with you if we did that?"

When she put it that way, "It would give May great pleasure," how could he refuse? He'd look like a terrible person if he said no. Reluctantly, he replied, "If my mother agrees, I guess that would be nice. Thank you."

"Wonderful! We'll plan to do that, then. Good day, Mr. Whylie." As she turned, he caught another whiff of her intoxicating scent.

"Good day, Miss Paul." Watching her walk out of the store, Andrew realized he was sweating and his heart was pounding too. He groaned. *What was I thinking? I should have found some excuse to get out of this, but it's too late now.*

Realizing that Mr. and Mrs. Boyle were looking at him in a curious way, he picked up the broom and attacked the floor with it, even though he had just swept it an hour ago.

What next? he thought miserably. *Now Miss Paul is talking to me about May and making plans. I can't do it. I can't go on looking like a fool around her. How can I get out of this? I wish she'd never come here in the first place!* In his heart, he knew that wasn't quite true. *But it's useless to dream. I have nothing to offer.*

CHAPTER TWENTY-SEVEN

Eavesdropping

Samantha and Briar sat outside on a patch of grass, scrubbing some of the new potatoes they'd be having for supper. The potatoes were so young and sweet that each girl was also nibbling on a raw one.

This morning, Mrs. Whylie had arrived to visit Mother once again, and she'd brought some delicious scones, which they'd all enjoyed with tea. Now she and Mother were still in the cabin, lingering over the last of the big pot of tea, and the girls could hear bits of their conversation drifting out the door. None of it was of particular interest to either of them until Samantha heard her own name. Then her ears pricked up, and although she'd been taught not to eavesdrop, she couldn't help herself. Trying not to alert Briar to what she was doing, she inched herself closer to the door.

Mother was saying, "Ever since they lost their father, I've worried more about keeping the children so far away from town and school and their friends, especially Samantha. She'll soon be twelve. Caleb's return has made me wonder if she might start to feel too isolated out here too, and if she might ever be tempted to leave like he did. The thought absolutely terrifies me. I couldn't bear to go through that again, not knowing where one of my children was."

After a brief silence, she added, "I can't thank you enough for stepping in and helping them get to school."

When Caleb had come home from the Whylie farm recently, he brought the news that the Whylies had acquired a buckboard wagon and Mrs. Whylie had kindly suggested that if the Lawson girls could walk as far as the farm, she would be pleased to drive them the rest of the way to school with May. This had been a very welcome offer, graciously accepted. Now all three girls were going to school—a dream come true for them and their mother.

Mrs. Whylie's kind voice replied, "I know there are many memories for you here. You and Mr. Lawson worked so hard homesteading, clearing the land, and planting crops. This is also where some of your children were born. As I say, many happy memories, but some sad ones too, I know. I wonder . . . do you ever think about leaving? Maybe it's time to think about moving into the village or even returning to Toronto. I know how hard it must be for you alone out here. It's an exhausting way of life, working from sun-up to sundown, and without a man . . . I don't know how you keep going."

Leaving? Toronto? Samantha was shocked to hear Mrs. Whylie's words. Of course, Mother had mentioned the idea at times, but to hear Mrs. Whylie suggesting it made it seem more real.

"Like you, I've never been afraid of hard work," Mother replied, "but we don't seem to be making any progress. We're in worse shape than ever without the money my husband was able to make in the lumber camps, and I certainly can't hunt and fish like he did, though goodness knows, I've tried! I keep thinking that maybe in a few years Caleb will be able to provide for us as well as his father did, but can we afford to wait that long? And looking ahead, someday he'll want to marry, and then he'll have to provide for a family of his own as well. I certainly don't want the girls and me to be an added burden to him."

"I'm sure Caleb would never look upon you as a burden, my dear," Mrs. Whylie said reassuringly. "And this isn't a decision to be made lightly, of course, but if you were to decide to sell the farm and either move into the village or return to Toronto, it might be wise to do it before winter arrives.

That's just two or three months away. It doesn't give you much time."

"I know you're right. It's not easy to think about, but I'll have to make a decision, and sooner rather than later. I didn't feel we could leave when we didn't know what had happened to Caleb. I wanted to be here if he ever came back. And thank heaven, he did."

"Yes," replied Mrs. Whylie, almost too softly to be heard. "Thank goodness he did."

As the topic changed to something less interesting, Samantha stopped listening. She rather regretted her eavesdropping now. She was upset by what she'd heard, and the old confusion she always felt returned when Mother mentioned the possibility of leaving. She didn't know if she wanted to leave her home, but she didn't know if she wanted to stay, either.

Oh, why did Father have to die? If he was here, everything would be better, she thought angrily. But somewhere deep in her heart she heard a little voice saying, "No, it wouldn't. Even when he was alive, things were getting harder all the time. Maybe we'd have had to leave anyway."

It was the first time she had ever acknowledged that fact, and in a way it made her feel a little better.

CHAPTER TWENTY-EIGHT

Keeping Secrets

In fading daylight, Samantha sat by a window mending a pair of Caleb's trousers. He'd be coming home again tomorrow, and she badly wanted to talk to him about so many things, not just the conversation she'd eavesdropped on that morning. Another important issue was weighing on her mind.

She felt miserable and sensed that her mother was picking up the signs that something was wrong, yet Samantha didn't want to discuss her problem with her mother. In a way, that made her feel even worse, for they had always been able to talk about anything. Casting a guilty glance across the room to where her mother sat, she was rewarded with a fond smile. *Can she read my mind?* Samantha wondered.

School had resumed three weeks ago, and she'd been so excited when she'd first heard about the new teacher. She'd always loved school, and while it had been closed she missed her classmates, particularly the three girls she considered her best friends.

But now everything was different. It wasn't just that there was a different teacher; that was fine, for she liked Miss Heather Paul. No, the problem was that Samantha's friends had changed in the past year. Two of them, Amy and Arlene, were already twelve. Victoria was still eleven like Samantha.

These three had always called her Sam in a friendly, teasing way because Samantha was such a tomboy, and she didn't mind the nickname. But now the way they said it felt meaner, as if they were making fun of her. She couldn't understand why. She knew she was a tomboy, and she didn't care; she enjoyed being more adventurous than the other girls and not being afraid of snakes and spiders. She loved going fishing. *Why did they make such a fuss about it?* she wondered.

They had also started making fun of her mop of curls. *Who cares if I hate brushing it? I don't. And now they're too prissy to play games at recess, in case their dresses get a tiny bit dirty! What's that all about? It's only a little dirt!*

Samantha clenched her teeth; she was so frustrated, she could spit. *Ew! How unladylike!* She could imagine the appalled looks on her friends' faces if she ever did spit.

"Something funny, dear?" her mother asked with a smile, and Samantha was startled to realize she had actually giggled out loud at the image of her disapproving friends.

"Oh, just something that happened at school. It's nothing, really."

She made a show of examining her stitching so she didn't have to say more.

Worst of all, they're always talking about boys. Boys! Why? She thought about the boys at school, puzzling this over. *They're all just a bunch of scrawny, silly pests! All boys are pests, even Caleb sometimes.*

With a resigned sigh, Samantha accepted that she was somehow out of step with her old friends. She didn't care much about being out of step, though; she certainly didn't want to behave as silly as they did. However, a strange sense of loss cast its unwelcome shadow over her; it was as if her old friends had gone away, and although they bore the same names and appearance complete strangers had replaced them.

She had no one to talk to about this, but she wondered if Caleb might understand since he was older. *Maybe when he was my age, his friends also changed. Could that be the reason he left home? Was he so unhappy he decided to run away?* She had never asked, but maybe tomorrow she would.

CHAPTER TWENTY-NINE

Back to School

Samantha jumped off the Whylies' wagon, followed by her sisters and May. She stopped and watched as Mrs. Whylie turned the wagon around, flicked the reins, told her horse to "Gee up!" and went back down the road at a lively clip. She would return at the end of the day to take the girls home.

Turning toward the schoolhouse, Samantha could just make out through the dusty windows the form of Miss Paul watching her students arrive. The girls all waved and were rewarded by their teacher's wave in return.

When the bell rang and they filed in, the room was already cozy from the fire the teacher had lit to relieve the early morning chill. Miss Paul was very popular with her students. It wasn't just that she was young and attractive; she had a happy manner that enlivened their days.

Samantha noticed how Miss Paul had made a thoughtful attempt to brighten up the bare classroom with bunches of field flowers placed in glass jars. Today, a lace collar and cuffs complemented the teacher's dark blue dress, and a small black-and-ivory cameo hung from a slim silver chain around her neck. *She always looks so colourful and pretty,* Samantha thought. It lifted her spirits. As her gaze swept the little classroom, she noticed the drab, often-patched clothes she and most of her friends wore, which stood in stark contrast to the teacher's lovely outfit.

With all grades in one room, the teacher was kept busy. She often asked the older students to help the younger ones with their lessons and was coming to rely on Samantha and May in particular, and even Briar to some extent. Samantha loved helping; she could see herself being a teacher one day, if things worked out and she could finish school. Sometimes, though, that seemed like a mighty big if.

The only part Samantha didn't think she'd like was the way some of the bigger boys were mouthy and tried to trick and deceive a new teacher, playing on her inexperience. However, Miss Paul seemed to be developing her own way of dealing with them, and so far no one had had to be expelled or even sent home. The worst bullies were often kept home to help in the fields anyway, which suited them because they didn't really want to be in school to begin with.

When the children ran outside for recess that morning, Samantha stuck close to May Whylie. She didn't feel up to any more teasing and silliness from her other friends. Only May seemed to be the same sweet person she had always been, and Samantha was glad for that. Briar also walked around the schoolyard with May; she too enjoyed her company. May was thirteen, more than a year older than the others.

Was May ever as silly as the other girls? Samantha wondered. *It's hard to imagine her behaving like that, but I haven't really seen her in the last year. Maybe she did, and she's changed again. Maybe it's a stage you go through when you're twelve. Oh, boy, I hope not!*

Rounding a corner of the school, they spied a group of girls huddled together in deep conversation. Amy, Arlene, and Victoria were among them. When Arlene looked up and spotted them, she broke away from the others and came running up, breathing hard with excitement.

"Did you hear?" she cried. "There's a witch in town! A real witch!"

"What are you talking about?" Samantha said. "There's no such thing as a witch."

"Is too!" Arlene drew herself up with self-importance, and her eyes shone with excitement. "It's Miss Shelley!" she exclaimed, enjoying the drama of revealing this impressive piece of news. Samantha and May exchanged doubtful glances but didn't say anything.

Arlene insisted, "She makes up potions! Victoria said!" Here she looked at Victoria for confirmation.

Victoria nodded. "She's got potions to make warts go away, potions to cure headaches, and all sorts of things."

Arlene giggled. "Victoria says she even makes a potion that can make someone fall in love with you! Her sister Elise tried it, and she's getting married!" Victoria nodded again.

"That's ridiculous," Samantha said. "My mother makes potions sometimes. She makes one out of mustard when we have colds, and she's not a witch!"

Arlene was miffed. "Maybe she is!" When she saw Samantha getting angry and ready to defend her mother, she relented. "Oh, don't be silly. My mother makes mustard plasters for colds too. It's not the same thing at all. Miss Shelley makes brews with plants from her garden. She really is a witch. Also, Amy saw a ghost in that upstairs window one night when she was out late. It was carrying a candle and was all dressed in white, with long white hair! It was walking around up there."

Samantha noticed that Briar was taking this all in and looking scared. "For heaven's sake, Arlene. There's no such thing as ghosts either. You're just being silly. It was probably just Miss Shelley."

"Just wait, smarty. You'll see," Arlene retorted. "We don't go anywhere near her house, and if you come into town, you'd be smart to stay away from it too. She might put a spell on you." She and Victoria ran back to join their group before Samantha could say anything more.

May frowned. "Don't listen to them, Samantha. They're just trying to make trouble."

But a tiny seed of doubt had been planted. "You don't think it could be true, do you? Miss Shelley does look a bit like a witch. I saw a picture of one once, and she had a funny front tooth. So does Miss Shelley!"

"No. I don't believe for one minute there are real witches! They're just making it all up. It's silly."

Samantha nodded. "You're right." But as the day went on, she kept thinking about what Arlene had told her and wondered, *What if she's right and there really are witches? I'm not going near Miss Shelley's house anymore, that's for sure!*

***

For some reason, the school day seemed to pass so quickly that all of a sudden it was time for home. Just as the children were preparing to leave, Miss Paul called the Lawson girls aside. "I've been intending to make some visits on the weekends to meet my students' families, and I'd like to come and see you and your mother this Sunday, if it's convenient. Here's a note for you to take home to her." She handed it to Chantal, whose eyes were huge with surprise. "Will you make sure she gets it, please? You can bring her reply to school with you tomorrow."

Samantha was speechless. Chantal couldn't say a word either; she simply nodded in excitement. Finally, Samantha managed to say "Yes, ma'am. Thank you" before the three sisters ran out of the classroom and into the yard, where Mrs. Whylie waited.

"Hi, Mrs. Whylie!" Briar called.

"Hello, girls. Hope you've had a good day."

"Oh, yes, ma'am," Samantha replied as they climbed up into the wagon and settled in.

Chantal, clutching the precious note in her hand, waved it right in Mrs. Whylie's face. "My teacher is coming to my house! To my house! I can't believe it." Her eyes danced.

"Well, how lovely!" As Mrs. Whylie clicked her tongue, signalling her horse to head home, she couldn't stop smiling at Chantal's excitement.

***

After getting off the wagon at the Whylie farm, the girls trudged along the last part of the road until their cabin came into view. When Samantha spied

Mother standing in the doorway watching for them, she allowed Chantal to race ahead. The little girl was ready to burst with their news.

"Mama! Mama!"

"My, something's got you worked up! Out with it. I know you can't wait to tell me something."

Chantal hopped from one foot to another, almost dancing. "My teacher is coming! She's going to come here! On Sunday! She wants to meet you! My teacher is coming to my house!" Remembering the now wrinkled and dirty note clutched in her hand, she held it out to her mother.

Looking at her sisters for confirmation, she asked, "Isn't that right, Samantha?"

"Goodness me! This is a surprise." Mother looked at Samantha with questioning eyes. "Just give me a minute to read this, dear." After scanning the note, her mother looked up, smiling. "Well, that certainly is exciting. It will be lovely to meet Miss Paul. We'll have tea. Won't that be nice?"

"Could we make scones for when she comes, Mother?" Briar asked hopefully. "Please? And could we have some of our raspberry jam with them?"

"Now that's a wonderful idea."

Turning to Samantha and Briar, Mother became more serious. "Do you have any idea why Miss Paul wishes to visit? Is there a problem at school I don't know about?"

Samantha thought, *There sure is. All my friends have changed completely, except for May, and I hate it.* But to her mother she replied, "Miss Paul just said she was going to begin paying a social call to as many families as she can before winter comes. Just a short visit to meet our parents and discuss our progress, I guess."

"Well, we must put ourselves to some housecleaning on Saturday. We'll need to sweep and dust and tidy up for sure. Then we should all be able to enjoy ourselves on Sunday."

Samantha groaned. She wasn't looking forward to extra cleaning, even for a visit from Miss Paul. Then a more troublesome thought wormed its way into her head. *What if this isn't just a social call? What if Miss Paul really is coming to discuss a problem?* She couldn't imagine what sort of problem that might be, though, as hard as she tried. She didn't think she'd done anything wrong. Neither had Briar or Chantal. But there must be something, mustn't there? Her previous teacher had never visited the children's homes. This was most unusual.

CHAPTER THIRTY

Samantha's Questions

Caleb was tending to Bonnie, cleaning out her stall and feeding her, when Samantha entered the lean-to. Handing her a rake, he teased, "You know what they say, 'Many hands make light work.'"

"They also say, 'Too many cooks spoil the broth,'" she retorted.

Samantha made a few stabs at the muck, then stopped. "Miss Paul sent a note home for Mother. She wants to come for a visit on Sunday."

Caleb gave Samantha an appraising look. "You don't seem too happy about that. Something wrong at school?" He stared at her a moment, then demanded, "Did you get into some kind of trouble?"

"No. I am not in some kind of trouble!" she shot back. It occurred to Samantha that this was the perfect opening for what she wanted to talk to her brother about, so she tried to calm down. Still, she hesitated. She didn't exactly know where to begin, but it was now or never because she had Caleb to herself, for a little while anyway.

"It's not exactly school. I still like school . . . and I love Miss Paul."

"Well, that's good. What's wrong then?"

"It's . . . it's my friends, Arlene and Amy and Victoria. Something's wrong with them. They've changed."

"Aren't they being nice to you?"

"They're all right. They're not really being mean or anything. They're just . . . different, and I don't like it."

"I have no idea what you're talking about, Samantha."

"Well, I don't know how to explain it, but it's like now that some of them are twelve, they think they're big stuff. They're suddenly all prissy and worried about getting their dresses dirty, and they don't want to do fun stuff anymore, like play Fox and Goose or Blind Man's Bluff. And don't even suggest catching frogs! They just sit around and talk about all kinds of boring stuff like hair ribbons and ringlets and, and boys! Ugh! It makes me sick. It's like they're very different people this year."

Caleb smiled. "Can't help you there. Girls are a mystery to me. Maybe when you're twelve, you'll understand it. Maybe you'll change too."

"Never! What a horrible thing to say!" She turned to leave.

"All right, all right, calm down. Sorry. Look, I don't know what's going on. Why don't you ask Mother?"

"She won't understand! Besides she's got bigger problems to worry about right now than my friends at school."

After a pause, she quietly asked, "Caleb, does that happen to boys too? Do they change like that all of a sudden? Did your friends change? Is that why you left home?"

Caleb looked at his forlorn sister. She wondered if he felt sorry for her, but now she had asked him the big question: Why had he left home two years ago? He must have known that eventually he'd have to try to explain it properly to someone, but he probably hadn't expected that person would be Samantha.

He drew a big breath and sighed. "Let's get out of here. We can walk a bit. Maybe I can explain it, and maybe I can't, but I'll try."

They headed down a narrow path into the woods and after a few minutes found a fallen log to sit on.

Although Samantha had been terribly eager to hear Caleb's story, she now made herself wait patiently while he gathered his thoughts. She knew this was something very important to him, and she didn't want to rush him. But now that he was actually ready to tell his story, she wasn't sure she wanted to hear it. She was nervous about what he might reveal.

CHAPTER THIRTY-ONE

Caleb's Story

"You want to know why I left home." Caleb shifted a bit on the log to get comfortable, stared at the ground for a few seconds, and then looked up at Samantha. "I really don't know if I have an answer. Back then I was just plain tired of working in the lumber camp with Father and then trying to clear the land here and put in crops and everything. I didn't have many friends. It seemed like work, work, work, all the time. Like it would never end. I've had a lot of time to think about it since then, of course. And in a way, I think I'm a bit like Father; he left England on a great adventure to come here. And I wanted to see some different places, too."

Samantha gulped. She had been a little nine-year-old then with no idea of how hard things must have really been for her brother. She looked into his serious eyes and saw the pain he still felt, but she didn't speak because she didn't know what to say.

Caleb looked away, perhaps embarrassed. He studied the ground at their feet. Picking up a long twig, he began absent-mindedly drawing lines and circles in the earth before taking a deep breath and resuming his story.

"I wanted something to happen, but I didn't know what. I couldn't tell Father or Mother because I didn't know what to say. I didn't want to complain because Mother seemed almost worn out. Father was feeling low too. Nothing was working out the way he thought it would. He probably thought that by then he'd have a good farm going and maybe a hired hand. He was likely just as fed up as I was.

"Sometimes I'd hear him talking to Mother. He'd tell her he was sorry he'd dragged her all the way from a nice home in the city to this hard life up here. She always said she was perfectly happy being here, of course, and that things would look up soon. But they never did. I guess I thought if I left they'd have one less mouth to feed, one less person to worry about. What did I know? Probably all they did was worry about me after I'd gone. I should have left a note, but I didn't know what to say. I was afraid they'd try to find me, so I just took off and ran as far as I could."

Caleb was silent as his eyes roamed the sun-dappled canopy of trees above them. Samantha wondered if that was all he had to say. If so, she'd be disappointed; she wanted to hear more about where he'd been for those two years.

Still looking up at the gently swaying trees, he resumed. "That first day on the road, I was worried someone would recognize me, but I was also excited because I was on an adventure, you know? Then night came and I was freezing. It was April, remember? Still a bit like winter. I hid in barns a lot, but it was still very cold and uncomfortable. I left here without any food too. It was a couple of days before I got so desperate, I knocked on a door. I must have looked like I was on my last legs. Someone felt sorry for me and invited me in to get warm and have a good meal."

Samantha was shocked to hear all of this, but still she didn't interrupt.

"It's true what the grown-ups are always saying: life isn't easy anywhere. I didn't want to believe it, but it's true, and some places are a lot worse than anything around here. I hitched rides on wagons, but mostly I walked. I said I was older than I was to get a bit of work here and there. Finally, I thought I'd struck gold when they hired me for a job in the mine, but it was the worst place I've ever seen. That's what hell must be like.

"I thought I'd have to stay there forever. I didn't know what to do next—I couldn't go home. After a while, Madame Laframboise, my landlady, had a talk with me. I was boarding at her house. She persuaded me my family was probably worried sick and would be so glad to see me, that they'd forgive me for running away. She said that's how she'd feel if I were her son." He paused again and looked at Samantha. "She was right, wasn't she? Except it was all too late. Father was gone. I was too darn late."

Caleb hung his head. Together they sat in silence for several minutes. Then Samantha gave her brother a big hug and said, "I'm sorry, Caleb. I didn't know it was so terrible for you. I'm glad you came back. We all are. And Father would be too. I know he would." She decided now wasn't a good time to bring up the conversation she'd overheard between their mother and Mrs. Whylie. It could wait.

They began to go back to the cabin, each lost in their own thoughts.

"I think you should tell Mother what's bothering you, or maybe tell Miss Paul," Caleb said. "They'd understand about the other girls. After all, they were your age once upon a time." And then he smiled and said, "Can you picture Mother being eleven or twelve years old? I can't imagine her ever being that young."

"Neither can I, but she must have been. It's strange to think about your parents actually being children, isn't it?"

Then a sudden thought made her laugh. "Little Miss Beetroots! That's what she said her brother called her because of her reddish hair. I bet she really hated that! Little Miss Beetroots!"

CHAPTER THIRTY-TWO

Preparing for a Social Call

On Sunday morning, Mother and Briar made scones while Samantha prepared a substantial pot of oatmeal for breakfast. Then Mother insisted Caleb get more buckets of water from the creek. It would take a while to heat up enough for them all to have baths and wash their hair.

"But I don't want a bath," Chantal pleaded. "I'm not dirty! And I hate it when you wash my hair. It gets all tangled, and it hurts."

"I'm with her," Caleb muttered. "I don't need a bath either. I was in the creek the other day. I'm fine."

"Oh, no!" Mother was adamant. "We're all going to bathe today, and that includes washing your hair, Chantal. And Caleb, being in the creek the other day doesn't count." She wrinkled her nose. "Believe me, you need a bath today!"

"But Mama," Chantal began.

"No buts about it! You two might not enjoy baths now, but believe me, one day you will. Then you'll think they're such a luxury, you won't ever want to get out of the tub."

"You always say that, Mother," Caleb said with a sigh. "One day this or one day that. You say that about a lot of things."

"That's because I'm older and just a little bit wiser." His mother smiled. "Now let's get that water. Samantha and Briar and I are actually looking forward to our baths."

"I'll get the tub." Briar went outside and struggled to lift the large metal tub from its hook on the rear wall of the cabin. Once inside, she placed it behind the curtain in Mother's alcove so everyone could have some privacy.

The tub was big enough for two small children, so Chantal and Briar shared the first bath, using the lye soap their mother made herself, which was rough but did the job. Chantal enjoyed splashing around with Briar a bit too much, and soon Mother had to get cross with them, as the floor was soaked.

Samantha was next. Like her mother, she really enjoyed relaxing in the tub, as a rule. Soaping herself up felt luxurious, and not many other things did in her family's life. Today, however, she was nervous about her teacher's visit, and the water was cooling quickly, so she jumped in and out in no time.

When Samantha was finished, Caleb threw out the dirty water and mopped the floor again. Mother heated more water for the last two baths. After that, they hung the big tub back on its hook until the next bath time.

Around one o'clock in the afternoon, they heard a buggy bouncing along the rough road, and Chantal squealed with excitement. Samantha felt butterflies in her stomach. She looked at Briar, who was being very quiet. *She's worried too,* Samantha thought. *I hope nothing's wrong, that this really is just a social call.*

Taking a deep breath to calm her butterflies, she crossed the fingers of both hands and followed her family outside to greet their visitors.

CHAPTER THIRTY-THREE

Tea and Scones for the Teacher

Miss Paul was not alone in the buggy. Caleb whispered to his mother, "That's Dr. Paul with her."

"Oh, dear." Mother seemed flustered at the appearance of an unexpected second guest and busied herself tucking a wisp of hair back behind Briar's ear, straightening Caleb's collar, and smoothing her own skirt. But she kept a smile on her face while the introductions were made and graciously invited Miss Paul and Dr. Paul into the cabin for tea.

"Thank you, Mrs. Lawson. Tea would be most welcome." The young woman smiled.

Her father added, "Yes, indeed, thank you, Mrs. Lawson. It was a dusty ride."

Caleb helped Dr. Paul remove Armon's harness and hitch the horse to a post where he could graze. As they walked toward the small log cabin, he noticed the doctor taking a quick glance around the clearing, as if assessing the situation. *Miss Paul probably told him Father's gone and Mother and the girls have been alone out here because I ran away.* Shame overwhelmed Caleb as he saw clearly, for the first time, the signs of neglect a visitor would spot immediately.

It must all seem so poor! The adjacent small field had been cleared to some degree but still had a great many tree stumps that needed to be pulled, and weeds and bramble were regaining ground. The stacked pile of logs beside the cabin door was pitifully small for this time of year, nowhere near enough to get the family through the winter. His eyes moved to the roof. *I tried my best with that chimney, but it's still crooked!* Caleb felt embarrassed for his mother. *Has she noticed Dr. Paul taking stock too?* he wondered. *If she has, she's not letting on.*

"I see you've been busy building up your woodpile." Dr. Paul smiled. "I'm sure your mother's grateful to have you back, for many reasons."

Caleb returned the smile, and his spirits lifted just a little at the kind words.

Inside, a pleasant surprise awaited the guests. Beatrice Lawson had opened her big trunk of precious items and removed several pieces of china and silver utensils, as well as a handsomely embroidered tablecloth. She laid the table with the pretty cups and plates in a floral pattern and shining silver cutlery. A large glass jar served as a vase for a bouquet of daisies.

"How lovely!" exclaimed Miss Paul. "What beautiful china!"

"Thank you. It was a wedding gift many years ago, and it's so nice to have an opportunity to use it."

"And such a beautifully stitched cloth. Someone spent many hours embroidering this."

"My mother did. Another wedding gift."

There weren't quite enough chairs, so Caleb had already brought in a small, smooth tree stump for himself to sit on. It was actually quite comfortable. Chantal would sit either on her mother's lap or cross-legged on the floor, which suited her just fine. She was too bouncy a child to sit for long on a chair anyway.

After everyone had taken their places around the table, Mother poured the tea and served the delicious, warm scones and jam.

Caleb noticed his mother surreptitiously observing their guests more closely as she served them. He tried to see them through her eyes. Heather Paul, tall and elegant like her father, seemed very young to be a teacher. She wasn't much older than he was. He thought her fair hair and exquisite green eyes were enchanting, and when she glanced his way and bestowed a sweet smile on him, he felt himself turning red in the face and was horrified that the others might notice! The young teacher was brimming with enthusiasm and perhaps just a bit of nervousness too. That was understandable. He thought she must resemble her late mother, as Dr. Paul's hair was darker. His kindly blue eyes and smile displayed his pride in his daughter, and in contrast to her, he exuded a quiet calm.

Miss Paul inquired, "Where are you from originally, Mrs. Lawson? I hope you won't mind my asking. I'm so interested in learning about the families of my students."

"I don't mind your asking at all. My family is from Toronto. My father practised law. His office was on Jarvis Street, and our home was just around the corner. My late husband, though, came from the old country—Leicester, to be precise."

"It's a very long way from a city in England to Lake of Bays," said Dr. Paul. "Your husband must have had quite a sense of adventure."

"He did, sir. But the two of you have also come a long way to settle here. Niagara-on-the-Lake is such a pretty town, I would have thought it difficult to leave."

"Do you know Niagara?" asked a delighted Miss Paul. "Most people have heard of it, of course, because it was the first capital of Upper Canada, but not many people from these parts, or even from Toronto, have travelled there."

"My husband and I took an extended trip to Niagara Falls and the area after our wedding. I imagine the town has grown since then."

Caleb and his sisters all looked at each other in surprise. This was a story about their parents they hadn't heard before. "You've seen Niagara Falls, Mother?" he asked. "What are the falls like?"

"Huge and wondrous and awe-inspiring." Mother smiled as she thought back. "The roar of all that rushing water is so loud that sometimes you have to shout to be heard, and if you get too close to the edge of the gorge, you'll get wet from all the spray."

"That sounds like fun," said Briar.

"Can we go to see them?" asked Chantal.

"They're a very long way away, dear, but you never know. Perhaps someday, when you're grown up, you'll have the opportunity to see them too. I hope so."

The light conversation continued into the afternoon. "I must say, I hadn't realized how much I've missed times like this over the years," Mother exclaimed. "It's delightful enjoying a cup of tea with such pleasant company on a Sunday afternoon." Caleb thought his mother seemed brighter and less tired than usual; some of the lines in her face had softened. She caught his eye and beamed, as if to say, "I'm so glad you're here!" Caleb had to look away; he was overcome with emotion. Not for the first time he thought, *I really did the right thing, coming home.*

Heather Paul and her father returned the compliment. "This has been completely charming, Mrs. Lawson. We've so enjoyed meeting you," Miss Paul said.

"Yes, it has," Dr. Paul added. "It can't be easy for you living out here, but"—he stopped and smiled at the four children—"you should be proud of your family."

Hearing his mother praised made Caleb feel happy for her, even though she blushed and tried to dismiss the kind words. It was also obvious how proud his sisters were to have their teacher and her father visiting their home. That remarkable afternoon, their eyes shone with that pride, and they looked as if they were floating on air.

As the guests prepared to depart, Mother asked, "Miss Paul, are you pleased with the children's progress at school or is there something we need to work on?"

"No need to worry there. I'm more than satisfied with your girls. Not only are they doing well, but they're also well behaved. I enjoy teaching each of them."

"Thank you. I'm happy to hear that."

Caleb watched his sisters' faces light up. Then Miss Paul spoke again. "Might we just take a little stroll, though, Mrs. Lawson? There are one or two small matters I'd like to discuss with you."

Samantha was puzzled and began to worry again. *One or two small matters? What does that mean? Miss Paul just said we're all doing well. She even said she enjoyed teaching us. So what could she possibly want to tell Mother in private?*

Before she could get too worked up, Dr. Paul interrupted her thoughts. "Well, children," he said, smiling at them all, "while the ladies are talking, how would you like to show me around the farm?"

CHAPTER THIRTY-FOUR

Conversations

Caleb rode in the Pauls' buggy as it bounced and rocked down the road. He had been happy to accept their offer of a ride back to the Whylies' farm. Samantha watched along with her sisters and mother, and just before a bend in the road took the buggy out of sight, both Caleb and Miss Paul turned to give one last cheerful wave.

Everyone returned their waves and then just stood there for another minute, as if reluctant to let their visitors go. Finally, Mrs. Lawson turned to go inside, saying, "What a lovely young woman. You're very fortunate to have her as your teacher."

As she helped her mother tidy up, Samantha couldn't help worrying again. *What could Miss Paul and Mother have been talking about?* She knew she couldn't ask just then, with Briar and Chantal around. *I'll wait 'til they're in bed,* she decided. *Or Mother might say something before then. I hope so.*

She decided to try to put the subject out of her mind for a while, if she could. "I wish they could have stayed longer," she said with a sigh.

"Yes," her mother agreed. "It was a lovely visit."

Picking up one of the pretty china teacups, Samantha thought she'd never touched anything so lovely and delicate. It made her wonder about the life her mother had led before coming here to the woods. "Mother, did you and Father use these dishes every day?" she asked.

"No, dear. These were our good dishes for Sunday dinner or when we had guests. We had a sturdier set for every day."

"Two sets of dishes?" Samantha couldn't believe it.

"Did you have lots of guests and parties?" Briar wanted to know.

"Not lots, but from time to time. It was different living in the city. People lived closer to each other, and it was easier to get together. The stores were also close by, and they had a greater selection of groceries." Mother looked wistful as she remembered. "We actually had milk delivered to our door, and a man came by regularly with his cart piled high with fruits and vegetables for sale."

"Wouldn't that be wonderful!" Briar said dreamily.

"It sure would," said Samantha as she swept the floor. "Wonderful."

Samantha had great difficulty imagining such a life of plenty; to her, it seemed unbelievable. *But Mother doesn't tell lies, so she and Father must have lived just like a princess and her handsome prince in a fairy tale.* It hadn't lasted, though. Before long, their adventurous father, the young Englishman Jarvis Lawson, had easily persuaded his beautiful "princess" Beatrice Hurst to join him in his dream of receiving a government land grant and farming in the north.

Later, Samantha slipped into her mother's room, where her parents' wedding photograph sat on a shelf. She examined the faces of the handsome young couple, fairly beaming with happiness and aglow with the promise of an exciting life ahead of them. *They seem like two strangers; I can't believe they're really my parents.*

Looking at the picture made Samantha deeply sad, and it wasn't just that she missed her father so much. There was something more. She couldn't figure out what until she realized that all the bright, golden dreams of that happy bride and groom, her mother and father, had become tarnished by the almost impossible task of building a farm in this harsh place.

When Samantha returned to the main room, her mother was sitting, head bowed, and looking at her hands. She was quiet, and when she spoke, her voice was so soft that she almost seemed to be whispering to herself.

"Yes, it would be wonderful to have those conveniences again, but those days are long gone. We were living in a privileged world and didn't realize it or appreciate it—we were so young. We thought we could have a happy life here too, although it would be a very different kind of life. And we might have, we almost did, but . . ."

The sentence remained unfinished. In her heart, Samantha knew how it would go: "Then your father died."

With a sudden shake of her head, as if to rouse herself from a dream, her mother stood up and added, "Maybe it's time now for another change."

***

That evening, when Chantal and Briar were in bed, their mother put an arm around her eldest daughter and said, "Samantha, I can see something's been bothering you for a while now. You're not your usual happy self, and I'm worried about you. Is there anything you want to tell me, dear?"

"No. Nothing's wrong. Everything's fine."

"Miss Paul has also noticed that you don't seem to be enjoying school as much as you did at the start. She wonders if it has something to do with your friends. Have you had a falling out?"

"No!" Samantha's denial was quick. *So that's what Miss Paul wanted to talk about! I was worried it might be something more serious, but I couldn't imagine what.* Now she felt a great relief. *I'm not in any kind of trouble! But I don't want to talk to Mother about this. I don't know what to say.*

"Well, dear, something must be going on. You seem worried and unhappy. I'd just like to help, if I can."

"It's nothing."

Her mother looked at her thoughtfully for a minute. Then she said, "You know, I've always thought that a boy's life must be a lot less complicated than a girl's."

Samantha was startled. *What a strange thing to say!* She wondered where this conversation was headed.

"I don't know for sure, of course, never having been a boy." Her mother smiled. "But I have always found boys to be quite straightforward about things. My experience with some girls about your age is that they seem to grow up faster than boys, and that's not easy. Some of them become more self-conscious and confused about certain things than they were when they were little girls. Your sisters, for example, are completely unaware of how pretty they are, and they don't seem too concerned about how they look or dress. But sometimes older girls attach too much importance to those superficial things."

Samantha was listening intently but trying to look as if she weren't. "My brother Wesley used to tease me all the time about being a bit of a tomboy," her mother continued. "But some of the girls were even worse teasers. It was confusing—one day it was all right to be a tomboy, and the next day it wasn't. Some of my friends became quite the proper little ladies and made fun of the rest of us. They managed to make our lives miserable for several months, until they found something else to occupy their minds. I survived it all, but it was quite hurtful and bothersome at the time."

Samantha didn't say anything, but she remained thoughtful. It was almost as if her mother could read her mind. *Maybe Miss Paul can too. Is it all so obvious?* Then she thought, *If the same thing happened to Mother, maybe it's just a stupid stage my friends are going through. If it only lasted several months with her friends, maybe that's what'll happen with mine. Boy, I hope so! I've had enough of this stupid stuff!*

"There's nothing wrong with being a tomboy, Samantha. I always thought it was a lot more fun than being too fussy about things."

"But you're not a tomboy anymore. You're a mother."

"Well, in time I guess we all have to grow up a bit, but even a mother can still be a bit of a tomboy at heart. Part of me always has been. Maybe that's why when your father proposed this adventure of leaving the city and farming up here, the idea appealed to me. I didn't mind roughing it with him. We had some difficult times, that's for sure, but we also had some wonderful ones I wouldn't have missed for all the tea in China."

Samantha noticed that her mother's eyes now shone with happy memories, and she was glad. So many times lately she'd worried about the dark circles under them and the fatigue Mother couldn't quite hide.

She considered what her mother had just said about the tomboy in her that had enjoyed the challenge of coming to Muskoka and roughing it. *I never had a problem with being a tomboy,* Samantha realized. *It's the other girls who have the problem.* Then a happy thought came to her. *And just maybe it's the tomboys who have more fun and adventures*!

CHAPTER THIRTY-FIVE

Catching Dreams

Caleb was astonished to see Dr. Paul's buggy pull up the following Sunday. His mother looked equally surprised when she stepped out of the cabin.

"Good afternoon, Mrs. Lawson. Afternoon, Caleb," he said, nodding. "I've just been to the Murray place and thought I might stop by on my way home. Hope you don't mind."

"Not at all. You're most welcome, Dr. Paul. I hope it's nothing serious with the Murrays."

"No, no. Just old Mr. Murray is laid up with arthritis pretty badly and can't get around much these days. I can't do much about that except give him a few remedies I hope will ease his discomfort. He's almost ninety, you know, and really quite remarkable. I enjoy talking to him. Did you know he was there in 1837 when the Upper Canada Rebellion began? He was right there at Montgomery's Tavern in old York! He knew the leader, William Lyon Mackenzie. That's before you and I were born. He's like a walking, talking history book."

"No, I didn't know any of that. I imagine he's had quite an interesting life. May I offer you a cup of tea, Doctor?"

"That would be lovely if you have the time. I don't want to interrupt anything important you were doing."

"You aren't. After all, it's Sunday afternoon and a cup of tea seems just the right thing."

"Thank you." As he climbed down from the buggy, Dr. Paul asked, "Are your girls around? I don't see or hear them."

"They went fishing quite some time ago. They should be back shortly."

***

Returning with her sisters and their small catch, Samantha was excited to see the parked horse and buggy; company was always welcome. Since she recognized Armon, she knew their visitor was Dr. Paul, and perhaps her teacher as well. In the cabin, she was pleased to find the doctor having a cup of tea with her mother and Caleb.

"Well, here come the fishermen! I was hoping I wouldn't miss you," he said with a big smile.

The afternoon passed quickly, with many interesting things to talk about, even for the youngest. Chantal was intrigued by the mysterious items in Dr. Paul's black bag, and he took out a tongue depressor for her to play with, explaining how it was used. She immediately tried it out on Briar, causing her sister to gag.

"Enough of that!" Briar frowned.

Dr. Paul laughed and asked Briar if he might have a look in her mouth and show her how it was supposed to be done.

"It doesn't hurt," he explained, "and I can learn a lot just by looking in a person's mouth."

Briar obviously didn't want to say no to the doctor, so she let him look down her throat. She still gagged a tiny bit but not nearly as much as when Chantal had practically shoved the tongue depressor all the way down.

"Everything looks just fine," the doctor pronounced. "My daughter is concerned that you may not be feeling well, Briar, because you seem tired at school, but you look like a healthy girl to me. Do you get enough sleep? You should be getting at least ten hours a night at your age."

Mother answered for Briar. "I make sure she goes to bed early, Doctor, but I'm not convinced she goes right to sleep. Several months ago she was having a lot of nightmares, but she hasn't mentioned them lately."

Samantha had been watching closely, wondering whether or not she should speak up. She decided the time was right. Her sister needed help.

"She still has them most nights. She tries to stay awake so she won't dream, but she always falls asleep eventually, and when she has the nightmares, I can feel her kicking and thrashing around."

"Is that right?" Dr. Paul said. "Well, you know what to do with nightmares, don't you, Briar?"

Briar shook her head. "No."

"You feed them hay!" he said, laughing. Everyone else thought this was funny too, and Briar smiled.

"But monkeys don't eat hay!" she blurted out. Embarrassed, she looked down at her feet.

Samantha felt sorry for Briar. *Uh-oh! Here we go! Now her secret's out.*

"Monkeys?" Caleb looked confused, as did Dr. Paul.

Mother looked puzzled. "You talked about monkey dreams a long time ago, dear, but I thought they'd stopped."

Briar started to cry. "He's still here! The scary monkey comes in the window almost every night. I'm afraid to go to sleep, so I try to stay awake but I can't." She ran into her mother's arms and sobbed even more.

Caleb shot a questioning look at Samantha. Apparently, this was all news to him.

"Well, we'll have to see if we can come up with a cure to scare that monkey away," said Dr. Paul. "I will consult my medical texts. Maybe someone else has had the same nightmares and found a solution."

"Do you think so?" asked Samantha. "Do you think other people have bad monkey dreams too? Not just Briar?"

"It's quite possible, my dear. When I was a little boy, I often had bad dreams about clowns. I had seen some in a parade, and they frightened me. Can you imagine? I was afraid of clowns!"

"But doctors aren't afraid of anything."

"But I wasn't always a doctor. I was a little boy once upon a time. I know that's difficult to believe now."

Caleb chuckled; he admired the doctor's reassuring manner.

Mother rested her chin on the top of Briar's head and said softly, "She first mentioned these dreams right after her father passed away." Dr. Paul nodded thoughtfully to indicate he understood the significance of this statement.

"Is that when the monkey came, Briar? After your father passed away?" he asked.

"Yes, I think so," she replied, still sobbing a little and hugging her mother.

"Well, that's understandable, then," Dr. Paul said. "But we mustn't let it go on. We'll see what we can do."

He rose to leave, and then as if remembering something, said, "Mrs. Lawson, I wonder if I might have a private word with you?"

"Of course, Doctor." She followed him outside, closing the door behind her.

From the window, Samantha and Caleb observed an earnest conversation. "I wonder what's up?" Samantha asked her brother.

He shrugged. "I don't know. You got me."

Several minutes later, the doctor got into his buggy and waved goodbye. When their mother returned to the cabin, she was deep in thought but offered no explanation as to what had been said. Samantha and Caleb exchanged anxious looks, and Caleb went to the lean-to to find his toolbox and busied himself for over an hour. When he came in for supper, he was hiding something behind his back.

"Briar, this is for you. It might help you with your nightmares." And he held out a strange-looking circle, about the size of his palm, made from bent twigs and laced with twine in a pattern that resembled a spider's web. Hanging from it on another piece of twine was a large partridge feather.

"What is it?" asked Briar.

"I've never seen anything like it," said Samantha.

"It's called a dream catcher. When I was in Sudbury, my friend from Temagami made one to hang in our room. It's supposed to catch bad dreams. It might catch your monkey dreams if I've made it right. We could hang it in the loft by the window. What do you think?"

"What a brilliant idea!" his mother exclaimed. "It might be just the thing."

Briar nodded, quite entranced by the dream catcher. She couldn't wait to hang it up and gave her brother a huge hug.

Caleb was pleased. He hated to think of any of his sisters being so scared. *I'm their big brother. It's my job to protect them.* He didn't have his father's wisdom yet, but maybe someday he would.

CHAPTER THIRTY-SIX

An Offering of Hope

May's cheeks were bright with excitement as Andrew helped her jump down from Dr. Paul's buggy in front of the general store. This outing was an unexpected adventure for his sister: a ride into the village in an actual buggy instead of a buckboard, with the teacher she idolized and without either of her parents. Andrew could tell she felt quite special and grown up. Despite the number of years between them, he and his sister were very close, and he was touched that seeing him meant so much to her. She had always adored her brother and he, in turn, never wanted to do anything to disappoint her or let her down.

"Thank you very much, Miss Paul and Dr. Paul," May said politely.

"Yes, thank you. We'll see you later," Andrew added.

"We'll look forward to it." Miss Paul smiled at both of them.

"Take your time. I'm sure the two of you have lots to catch up on," her father added before signalling Armon to proceed home.

"How you've grown!" Mrs. Boyle exclaimed when May entered the store. Andrew was amused to see his sister blush.

"I thought we'd sit outside since it's still mild," he suggested.

"Take a few of these with you, then." Mr. Boyle put a few cheese biscuits into a basket and handed it to May.

"Thank you, sir," Andrew said, moved by the man's kindness.

They sat on the back steps of the store to chat. May was full of stories about school and her friends, and all the little intrigues he remembered from his own school days.

"I'm really worried because now that the harvest is over, some of the big boys have been sent back to school, and they're giving everyone a hard time, especially Miss Paul," said May.

"Yeah, I remember what that's like. They'd rather be anywhere else but school, so they try to cause enough trouble to get expelled."

"But Miss Paul is so nice, and they're so rude. I hope she doesn't get so upset she'll quit!"

Andrew felt sick at the thought of these bullies harassing the lovely teacher. She was young and inexperienced, just a couple of years older than most of them.

"I'm sure she knows how to handle bullies." He hoped he sounded convincing. "How are things at home?" he asked innocently. He wished he hadn't, as May began to list all the repairs and improvements their father and Caleb were making. As she went on, Andrew's mood darkened. He began to feel even more reluctant to try to get home for visits with his parents. He didn't think he could stomach seeing Caleb on the farm again.

At one point during May's gushing recital, he became so angry, he almost swore out loud but stopped himself just in time. *I can't let May see how furious all this talk of the Lawson kid makes me. It's not her fault I feel so rotten,* he thought. *And I'm not going to spoil her special day with my lousy mood.*

Andrew stood up. "Well, I guess it's time we go for dinner. It was nice of Dr. Paul to invite us. And lucky you, getting a ride into town in his buggy!"

"And he's going to drive me home too!" May's face lit up, and Andrew was glad to see her so happy, although the dinner invitation had distressed him. He felt terrified at the idea of having to make small talk and be sociable with Miss Heather Paul and her father. He was certain he'd make a fool of himself somehow, but as with their offer to bring May to town for a visit, there really had been no way to refuse their kind invitation. With great trepidation he set off with his sister, who remained blissfully unaware of how her brother was feeling.

At first, Andrew was so nervous he was barely aware of what he was eating, but as the dinner progressed, he was amazed to discover he was enjoying himself; the Pauls both made conversation easy. *This isn't as bad as I thought it would be.* He was beginning to relax when Dr. Paul said, "Andrew, I wondered if you'd have a moment to come into my office after dinner? There's something I'd like to discuss with you while you're here."

"With me?" Andrew tensed. "What?" He realized he sounded rude, but he'd been taken by surprise. What could Dr. Paul possibly want to discuss with him?

"Nothing to worry about," the doctor said. Perhaps sensing Andrew's tension, he added, "I thought you might tell me about your back. I don't know what happened, and there might be some way I can help."

Andrew had never talked about what happened to anyone. For him, that day marked the end of his active, healthy life and any real dreams he had for his future. Dr. Paul's sudden question made him feel trapped, like a rabbit in a snare, too terrified to think clearly or know what to say.

After an uncomfortable silence around the table, May spoke up and in all innocence described the dramatic event. With wide eyes, she said, "He was at the camp and a big, big log got loose from a pile and knocked him down." Here she stretched her arms as far as she could, forming a circle to indicate the size of the infamous log. "We didn't know anything about it, though, and then one day, the men brought him home in the wagon. Mama cried. He was in so much pain. Father was furious because the camp doctor told Andrew he couldn't do anything for him . . ." She stopped, perhaps realizing she had spoken out of turn.

Andrew was horrified to feel a flush creeping up his face. When he raised his eyes, May was staring at her plate and Miss Paul's face was white.

Dr. Paul's gentle voice was kind. "I'm sorry you've had to deal with such a terrible accident, Andrew. There's no need to talk further right now." Nodding to his daughter, he said, "I think we're all ready to enjoy the delicious apple pie Mrs. Lawson baked for us this morning."

Miss Paul, taking her father's hint, went to the warming oven, from which tempting aromas of cinnamon and nutmeg had been drifting into the dining room. She returned carrying a golden, flaky pie and a small jug of fresh cream to accompany it.

Andrew, thankful for the change of topic, rallied himself enough to enjoy three pieces. When there was nothing left of the tasty dessert, he and May took their leave. They both thanked their hosts for their hospitality, and everyone walked out to the buggy, where Armon stood hitched and ready to go. He had also had dinner; a bucket of oats lay empty on its side.

As Dr. Paul adjusted the horse's harness, he quietly spoke to Andrew. "Last year in Toronto, I learned about some new methods a few doctors are using to relieve back pain similar to yours. I don`t want to raise your hopes unnecessarily, but I'd like to examine you. There might be something I can suggest. I believe it's worth a look."

Andrew looked away; he couldn't bear the thought of disappointment if the doctor were proven wrong.

"Thank you, sir, but I'd just as soon not. And I couldn't go to Toronto for treatment anyway, so there's no point."

Dr. Paul didn't pursue the matter. He climbed into the buggy beside May, who was yawning as she waved goodbye to Miss Paul and Andrew.

As Andrew walked back to his small cupboard of a room in the rear of the store, his limp was more pronounced, reminding him he was quite tired; it had been a long day. The familiar pain shooting through his back caused him to grimace with each step. Momentarily, he began to think how wonderful it would be if Dr. Paul could help him find relief, but then he stopped, refusing to let his mind consider the possibility. *Can't afford the treatment anyway. Just have to accept that this is how it is. This is my life now. No point in thinking it could be any different.*

CHAPTER THIRTY-SEVEN

Caleb and Andrew

Despite his efforts, Andrew couldn't avoid running into Caleb now and then. If he managed to avoid him at the farm, the boy showed up at the store on an errand for his mother or Andrew's parents. The unsuspecting fellow was pleasant and friendly but looked completely unaware of how Andrew seethed inwardly at the thought of his working alongside his father.

Mr. and Mrs. Boyle had not confronted Caleb about the missing knife either, but they now kept a close eye on him whenever he entered the store. No one had said a word about the jail story Andrew claimed to have heard. *Not a single question! You'd think somebody would care about a possible thief or jailbird in the village!* Andrew's increasing frustration gnawed at him.

Today, he was home for a visit. Much as he'd tried to avoid it, he'd been unable to fend off his mother's requests to come home any longer, and finally his father had made the trip into town just to pick him up. The day was shaping up to be another scorcher, and just as he was leaving the heat of the kitchen, hoping to catch a breath of cooler air on the porch, he came to a halt. He was staring at Caleb Lawson.

Even though he'd braced himself for this, the sight of the boy here on the farm still struck Andrew with the force of a punch in the gut. Anger and frustration twisted his features. After a couple of moments' hesitation, he eased himself down to perch on the top step, where with narrowed eyes he followed Caleb's every move. *What's it going to take to get rid of you once and for all?* he thought, seething.

***

Caleb could sense unfriendly eyes following him.

He was well aware of the cold looks directed at him but couldn't understand the reason behind them. Andrew didn't speak to him unless he had to and seemed to dislike him. Caleb had tried talking to him about a few things and then given up. He wouldn't waste his time anymore.

Gathering up an armload of the firewood, Caleb headed up the porch steps to the Whylies' kitchen. The logs were piled so high, he could hardly see over them, just enough to make out the top of the open door where he was headed. Since Andrew was occupying most of the top step, he had to keep well to one side. On the top step, he felt the toe of his boot catch on something.

"Oh-h, no-o-o!" he groaned as he stumbled and went flying. Fighting to retain his balance on wobbly legs, he felt his fingers lose their grip on the logs. As each log hit the porch floor, it added to the thunderous clatter, which to Caleb's ears seemed loud enough to wake the dead.

A split second later, he lost his battle to stay upright and landed on some of the logs. It was not a soft landing: he knew there would be several painful bruises the next day. Caleb had the distinct feeling he'd tripped over something but couldn't figure out what had been in his way—until he caught a brief, triumphant look pass over Andrew's face before it reverted to its normal, unemotional expression.

"You dirty so-and-so!" he wanted to rage out loud at Andrew, but before he could say anything, Mrs. Whylie flung open the door, alarm written all over her face.

"Are you all right, Caleb?"

"I think so, ma'am." He stood up, gingerly stretching his legs and arms. "Nothing broken, far as I can tell. Guess I was overloaded." Caleb avoided looking at Andrew but noticed that Mrs. Whylie was regarding her son.

"Andrew! Help Caleb gather up the wood and stack it!" she ordered, then turned and went back into the house.

Her words shocked Caleb; Andrew did very little bending and lifting because of his back injury. But without protest, he bent to gather a few pieces of wood, letting out a sharp, involuntary gasp, then quickly trying to hide his pain behind a forced, rigid smile. By the time all the firewood was stacked beside the kitchen stove, Andrew's face was several shades paler. Grabbing a nearby chair, he dropped onto it.

Sensing tension in the kitchen that he'd prefer to avoid, Caleb stepped out to chop more wood, leaving Mrs. Whylie and her son alone.

***

Andrew watched as his mother took the boiling kettle off the stove and made a pot of tea. While she waited for it to steep, she kept silent and busied herself with tidying up the kitchen table. Only after she'd poured two cups of the brew did she sit down across from him.

He couldn't look at her but felt her eyes on him and thought, *She knows! She must have seen me stick my foot out when Caleb came up the steps.* He was overcome with shame and couldn't look at his mother.

"I'm disappointed in you, son. I thought you had better control of yourself than that, and I don't know why you dislike Caleb so much. Now don't look so surprised; I've been aware for some time how you feel about him. What's it all about? Has he done something your father and I should be aware of?"

Andrew hesitated; possibilities raced through his mind at lightning speed. *Should I tell her what I told the Boyles? That he probably stole the knife?*

Or that I heard he was in prison? She might believe me. He sighed. *But I simply can't lie to her.*

"No." Andrew spoke softly, still not looking at his mother.

"Well, then, what is it? Are you jealous of him for some reason? I can't imagine why you would be; he's only a fifteen-year-old boy who needs to earn money because he's lost his father. Your father needed help, and it's working out well for both of them."

"Father wouldn't need his help if I hadn't had that damn accident! It should be me out there working with him."

"Ah! So that's it, is it? Son, I know that terrible accident changed everything for you, but you mustn't let it make you bitter and nasty."

Her concerned eyes moved slowly from his face to a spot in one corner. He followed her gaze and wished he hadn't; his fiddle stood there like a silent rebuke.

For a few moments, neither spoke. When his mother broke the silence, Andrew thought his heart might break. Her tone was soft and wistful. "You've even lost your music, Andrew. You used to love to pick up that fiddle and play a little something nearly every day, and it gave all of us such pleasure."

When he didn't answer, she spoke with sudden urgency. "Listen, son, when Dr. Paul brought May home the other day, he told us he'd spoken to you about coming to see him for an examination. He seems to think there's something new that might help you. Have you gone yet?"

"No, Ma. There's no point. I can't go to Toronto for treatment, and it probably won't work anyway."

"Your father and I would like you to see Dr. Paul and at least hear what he has to say. You really haven't seen a good doctor. That so-called doctor at the lumber camp just looked you over and sent you home with no hope. Maybe there is hope. Please go and see Dr. Paul."

"Please, Mother, don't push it! I don't want to get my hopes up for nothing."

His mother reached out and took his hands in hers; her loving eyes searched his face. "Andrew, think what it might mean to be able to come back to the farm! Even if you can't be completely healed, perhaps the doctors could relief your pain enough that you could do some farm chores. Wouldn't that be better than what you're doing now? I know you'd rather be here. Just go to see Dr. Paul, and he'll tell you soon enough what he thinks can or can't be done. You're in too much pain, and from what I witnessed this morning it's changing you—and not for the better!"

This last comment hit Andrew hard, and he bowed his head. Ashamed by his mother's disappointment, he concluded the only way to make things better was to agree to see Dr. Paul. With a distinct lack of enthusiasm, he finally replied, "All right. I'll go."

"Bless you, son. I have a good feeling about this. Now please, go out there and apologize to Caleb. It's the right thing to do."

Andrew couldn't believe his ears. *Go out there and apologize? That was going one step too far!* He shook his head. "Ah, Ma, no. You're asking too much."

The steely look in her eyes told him she wouldn't accept no for an answer. With a dramatic sigh, Andrew let her know he was not happy about this request and took his time rising from the table and making his way outside. He was smart enough to know better than to let the door slam behind him.

***

Caleb was alarmed to see Andrew ambling toward him. *What now?* he wondered. Laying down the axe, he stood with his feet apart and hands on his hips, ready to defend himself if necessary.

Andrew wouldn't look him in the eye as he approached, but he reached out as if offering to shake hands. Caleb was wary and didn't respond. Instead, he flexed his hands, preparing to defend himself.

"Relax," Andrew said, still holding out his right hand. "Guess I lost my head for a moment. Won't happen again. Shake?"

Caleb hesitated, confused. Finally, with a hesitant "Guess so" he gave Andrew's hand a brief shake.

Andrew nodded as if to say, "Well, that's over with," and turned to mount the steps again.

As Caleb watched him go, he shook his head in amazement. *Sometimes,* he thought, *there's just no understanding some people.* But despite this unexpected show of goodwill, Caleb decided he wasn't ready to let his guard down around Andrew Whylie. *Got to stay alert around that one. Don't think I can trust him just yet.*

CHAPTER THIRTY-EIGHT

Threatening Rumours

"Buggy comin'!" announced Mr. Whylie. He leaned on his shovel and squinted. "Must be Doc Paul." Caleb turned to watch and recognized Armon pulling the familiar vehicle. Mr. Whylie lumbered down to the edge of the road as the doctor pulled up to a stop.

Caleb observed the doctor remove his hat and take a handkerchief from his pocket to wipe his brow. After speaking to Mr. Whylie for a few moments, Dr. Paul climbed down and began to walk toward Caleb. Mr. Whylie glanced in his direction, and then, without saying anything, walked toward the house. Caleb couldn't help but wonder what was up. He began to worry.

"Is something wrong, Doctor?" His words rushed almost ahead

of his thoughts. "Is it my mother?" Now he began to panic. "Are the girls all right?"

"Far as I know, everyone is just fine, Caleb. No need to worry. I'm not here on a medical matter."

Caleb felt relieved, but something still didn't seem quite right. Why would Dr. Paul want to speak to him?

"I'm here on quite another matter. I need to talk to you about something I've heard. It's a little distressing, and it needs to be cleared up."

"All right," Caleb replied anxiously and waited for the doctor to elaborate. He couldn't imagine what could be so distressing or important that the doctor would drive all the way out here to talk to him.

"Your mother might not have told you, but when I was there a couple of weeks ago, I had a chat with her about moving into town. She had confided in my daughter that she was thinking about it."

Caleb was surprised his mother had spoken to anyone outside the family about moving. He knew she had thought about it from time to time, but that was all.

"No sir. She didn't say anything about it, but I'm not surprised. Things aren't really going that well on the farm."

"So I understand." The doctor glanced off toward the farmhouse for a minute before turning back to Caleb.

"This isn't easy to say, Caleb, but I have to ask. I made enquiries in the village and learned that Miss Shelley was thinking of moving. I thought her house might suit your family, so I paid her a call.

"When I told her what I had in mind, she became rather evasive and reluctant to discuss matters. I'm afraid I pressed her a bit, and she finally told me she was hesitant about dealing with your family because of something she'd been told. A rumour, to be sure, but still . . ." The doctor hesitated.

"What is it, Dr. Paul?" Caleb braced himself.

As he replied, the doctor's keen eyes searched Caleb's face, watching for a reaction. "There seems to be a rumour in the village that when you were away you weren't in Sudbury working in a mine at all. You were actually in jail . . . for theft. I'm sorry, but I have to ask you whether or not this is true."

Caleb's jaw dropped. He stared at Dr. Paul, speechless. *In jail? Where would anybody get that idea? Jail? For theft?*

Finally, he managed to splutter, "No! It's not true! I wasn't in jail! I was in Sudbury! I can prove it if I have to. I can write to the mine owners, to my landlady, Madam Laframboise, to . . ." Agitated, he waved his arms around in frustration.

"It's all right, Caleb," the doctor said. "Calm down. I believe you, but I had to ask."

Caleb was pacing back and forth now; he couldn't calm down.

"But why would anyone think I was in jail? Where did that idea come from?"

"Who knows? Gossip is a strange and dangerous thing; stories grow out of all proportion to the truth, and busy tongues can do a lot of damage. Now that I have your word on it, I can do my best to quell this. I'll reassure Miss Shelley."

"Thank you, sir." Caleb was breathing hard.

Dr. Paul reached out and put a gentle hand on his shoulder, forcing him to stop pacing.

Caleb's mind was a jumble of thoughts about how this awful rumour might have started when an even more disturbing thought popped up. "I sure hope my mother doesn't hear about this!"

"If she does, I'm quite sure she'll take it in stride. She's a strong woman, and she knows her son well."

"But still, who would start such a rumour? Why would anybody bother spreading lies about me? I'm not that important! I'm nobody!" Caleb was still flustered, but now he'd become angry.

"I don't know how this story got started. I can't imagine you have any enemies. And try not to get too worked up; I believe you, and now I can put a stop to this before things get worse."

Caleb nodded.

"Now I think I'll drop in on Mrs. Whylie for a minute before I get back to my rounds."

Caleb watched the doctor cross the field toward the house. "I can't imagine you have any enemies," the man had said.

Until recently, Caleb hadn't thought he had any enemies either, but now he could think of one who had made it very clear he didn't like him and didn't want him working on the Whylie farm.

CHAPTER THIRTY-NINE

Confrontation

Caleb's agitation over the rumour festered, and more and more, he was convinced Andrew was behind it. He finally decided he needed to talk to him. Not wanting to create a scene on the farm, where Andrew's parents would be present, Caleb decided he'd have to go into the village.

It was another two days before an opportunity presented itself. Caleb finished his chores early and worked up his nerve to ask Mr. Whylie's permission to quit before his usual time. It wasn't easy; he felt guilty knowing he intended to confront the man's son, but it had to be done. He didn't understand what was going on with Andrew, but whatever it was, it had to stop.

"I have an errand in town" was all the explanation he offered. He tried not to give anything away with his expression. Above all, he didn't want to answer any questions from Mr. Whylie.

The farmer leaned on his spade and stared at Caleb, apparently taken aback by this unexpected request. He mopped his brow with a dirt-caked handkerchief and seemed to take forever thinking about his answer. All the while, Caleb was sweating from more than just the heat of the day.

"Well, all right for today, I guess" was the slow and grumpy response. "Just don't make it a habit."

"No, sir. I won't. Thank you." Caleb raced off before Mr. Whylie could change his mind or ask any awkward questions.

Once out of sight of the farm, he slowed his pace and pondered his situation. As anxious as he was to confront Andrew, he was also darned scared. *This could cost me my job. Could? It probably will if Andrew tells his parents, and why wouldn't he?*

The sun was a little lower in the sky, but its heat remained intense; salty sweat stung his eyes and blurred his vision. Coming to a stop in the middle of the road, he mopped his sweaty brow with a dusty shirt sleeve and thought, *Maybe I should just forget this. Turn around now and go back. I can learn to ignore Andrew. Besides, he shook my hand, didn't he? Said it wouldn't happen again.*

A worm of doubt wriggled in his brain. It seemed to say to him, "Don't be a fool. How can you trust him?"

"You're right. I can't," Caleb replied out loud. He resumed his pace. *How am I going to do this? What'll I say? What if he just laughs at me? He'll probably tell me to get lost. Then what?*

In this way, Caleb passed the miles until he found himself standing in front of the general store, still unsure how to proceed. Just as he'd been afraid of causing a scene in front of Andrew's parents, he wanted to avoid one when the Boyles or anyone else might be present; word would eventually get back to his mother. *There's enough gossip already. No need to cause any more. I just need to clear the air.*

Something urged him on, though; taking a deep breath, he took a step toward the door, deciding he'd just see how things developed. *I don't believe I can trust him,* Caleb thought repeatedly. *I have to do this.*

The cheerful little bell attached to the store's front door chimed as he entered. Mrs. Boyle made her weary way out from somewhere in the rear, smoothing a wisp of lank hair and tucking it behind her ear. The heat seemed to have wilted her; she flapped a hand in front of her red face like a fan.

"Afternoon, Caleb," she said listlessly.

"Afternoon, Mrs. Boyle. I'm looking for Andrew. Is he here?"

"Andrew? What do you want him for? If you need something, I can get it." Her tone was a bit sharp, and Caleb thought the heat must be making her crabby.

"I just need to talk to him for a minute, that's all." Caleb hoped the woman wouldn't ask any more questions. He was nervous enough without having to come up with more explanations. To his great relief, she seemed to accept his answer and nodded. "He's out back, taking a break. Hoping to get a breath of air, I guess, though I can't imagine it's any cooler out there," she said, pointing to the rear door. "Just go on back through here."

As Caleb passed her, she seemed to feel revived and become more alert. Her forehead creased with concern. "Is everything all right, Caleb? Nothing's happened at the farm, has it? It's not bad news, I hope?"

"No, no! Nothing like that." He was quick to reassure her but offered nothing further as he hurried toward the back door and flung it open.

In his haste, he charged right into Andrew, who sat perched on the top step, his back to the door. "What the?" the surprised fellow exclaimed. Caleb's weight propelled Andrew forward, headfirst toward the ground. Andrew's arms spun like a windmill as he fought for his balance. Instinctively, Caleb grabbed an arm and yanked so hard, they both fell backwards, Andrew landing on top of Caleb, pinning him down.

"What the heck do you think you're doing?" Andrew pushed himself partway off Caleb before a spasm of pain seized him, causing his body to go rigid briefly. Seeing Andrew's face contort in agony, Caleb felt a pang of sympathy for him and had to remind himself why he'd come. When the spasm passed, Andrew's eyes blazed with fury, no more than an inch or two from Caleb's face. "I oughta punch you out for that!"

"Let me up!" Caleb struggled for breath and wriggled and pushed until he was free of Andrew's weight. Once he managed to stand, he sagged against the building's wall, his chest heaving as he gulped in air.

Andrew pushed himself to his feet. The two stared at each other, the hostility between them so thick you could have cut it with a knife.

If he starts swinging, I could be in trouble, Caleb thought. *He's taller and packs more weight, but I'll take him on anyway!*

"I asked you a question," Andrew yelled. "What's the matter with you?"

"Me?" Caleb shouted back. "What's the matter with you? Spreading lies about me! What have you got against me, anyway? You've always got a chip on your shoulder."

"What are you talking about? I haven't done anything."

"What on earth is going on here?" an alarmed Mrs. Boyle demanded as she stepped out the door. "Are you two fighting? I won't have it! Explain yourselves." She looked first at Caleb, then at Andrew. "I'm waiting." Turning to Caleb again, she said, "Did you come here looking for trouble?"

He stared at Andrew. He didn't really want to go into everything in front of Mrs. Boyle, but if that's how it was going to be, he was just angry enough to speak up.

"Dr. Paul told me everyone's talking about me," he began. "They're saying I was in jail. I wasn't, and I want to set the record straight. I also know who started that rumour." He turned and glared at Andrew.

"I don't know what you're talking about!" Andrew said, clenching his fists as if ready to throw a punch. "You're crazy! Besides, why would I even bother? You're nothing to me, just some stupid kid who ran away from home. Who knows what you were really doing anyway?"

"Andrew!" Mrs. Boyle's sharp voice scolded. "I'm surprised at you. I've never heard you speak that way to anyone."

Andrew looked away.

Caleb opened his mouth to answer, just as Mr. Boyle appeared around the corner of the store. "What in blazes is going on back here?" he demanded. "Are you all right?" he asked his wife.

"I'm fine, but these two aren't! Something's going on here I don't understand."

"Andrew's trying to start trouble." Caleb turned to Mr. Boyle. "He's spreading lies, saying I was in jail. Miss Shelley's heard about it and says she doesn't want to rent her house to my mother! If Mr. Whylie hears it, I'll lose my job."

"Those are pretty serious accusations both ways," Mr. Boyle said.

"You're saying Andrew's spreading lies about you, and Andrew says you're lying about that. How's anybody to know who's telling the truth?" His eyes roamed from Caleb's face to Andrew's and back again. "I heard that rumour, Caleb, but I didn't think it could be true, so I didn't say anything about it." He turned to Andrew. "Seems to me I heard it from you, Andrew." He paused, giving Andrew a chance to respond. When there was no reply, Mr. Boyle continued, "As I remember, you said you heard it from some traveller passing through, asking about Caleb. You don't happen to remember his name, do you? Or where he was from?"

"No, sir."

"Well, then, seems to me there's no proof. I'd take Caleb's word over some stranger's just passing through—if there was such a stranger." This last part came out almost in a whisper.

"I surely wouldn't like to think you'd make something like that up, Andrew. That doesn't seem like you," Mrs. Boyle said, peering intently at the increasingly uncomfortable-looking young man.

"No, ma'am."

"I know he did!" Caleb spluttered. "For some reason, he's got it in for me." He turned his anger on Andrew. "What did I ever do to you? That's what I want to know."

A slight smirk played on Andrew's lips, then disappeared in a flash.

"I think you should get back to work, Andrew." Mr. Boyle's stern expression indicated this was the end of things for now. "And, Caleb, if I ever hear anyone mention that rumour, I'll make sure to squelch it. I believe I can take you at your word."

"Thank you, sir," Caleb said, breathing a sigh of relief.

"Besides, it would be a simple enough thing to prove, wouldn't it? A letter to the right government office is all it would take, if it became necessary." There was no mistaking the warning in this comment.

"Yes, sir."

"Now I imagine you'll be wanting to get home." Caleb knew that was an order, not a suggestion.

"Yes, sir," he repeated. Turning to leave, he grimaced at the storekeeper's wife. "Goodbye, Mrs. Boyle. Sorry if we upset you."

She acknowledged his apology with a curt nod.

What a fiasco! Caleb groaned to himself. He was disappointed that Andrew hadn't confessed but reassured that the rumour would be put to rest, eventually. *So it wasn't a complete waste of time, but what did I expect? That he'd go down on his knees and beg my forgiveness?* He almost laughed, except it wasn't the least bit funny.

With dragging footsteps and a sinking heart, he headed back to the Whylie farm. He blamed himself for what likely lay ahead. *I've probably just made things a whole lot worse. He's bound to tell his father about this. There goes my job!*

CHAPTER FORTY

A Family Meeting

Five days later Samantha carried home a note from school addressed to her mother. The three girls were naturally curious, and also a little nervous, as to why their teacher would be writing to her again, even though Miss Paul had seemed quite happy when she handed the note over and hadn't acted as if anything were wrong.

Mother sat down at the table to read it, and the girls stood by quietly, hoping for some indication of its contents, but after finishing it, all she said was "Hmm." Then she took the note to her room and came back empty-handed. She began asking the girls about their day at school; clearly, she didn't intend to satisfy their curiosity, which was immensely frustrating.

There were the usual after-school chores for everyone, and since this was a day Caleb was not at the Whylie farm, he was able to pitch in. Everything was accomplished more quickly.

During supper, Caleb was anxious to find out from Briar how the dream catcher was working. It hadn't helped the first night he gave it to her, and they had both been disappointed, but now she said it must be working because the monkey hadn't appeared in her dreams the past four nights. The adoring looks she gave her big brother made him happy and proud. He had felt so sorry for his troubled little sister, and he was pleased that he might have helped her, whether it was really the dream catcher's work or not.

"Will you make me a dream catcher, too?" asked Chantal. "Sometimes that mother bear comes in my dreams, and I want her to stop!"

Caleb assured her he would make another one, perhaps even that evening right after supper. However, when supper was over and he was preparing to get out his toolbox, their mother announced that she wanted to discuss something important with them all, so they remained in their chairs wondering what it might be. She excused herself, went to her room, and returned with the note from Miss Paul.

"Dr. Paul and Miss Paul know I've been concerned about staying here on the farm for another winter," she began. "Since your father passed away, the work has become too much, and I feel we're too far away from help should anything go wrong. We're also much too far from your school."

Caleb thought back to his conversation with Dr. Paul about Miss Shelley and the nasty rumours about himself in the village. He interrupted his mother's train of thought. "But where would we go?"

"That's the question," she replied. "I had intended to write to my cousin John in Toronto, but I kept putting it off and never did."

"Toronto?" Samantha piped up, a worried look on her face. "What would we do there? Everyone we know lives here."

"I realize that," her mother replied. "And that's why I've been thinking about moving into the village, or at least very close to it. Mrs. Whylie and I discussed it, and I mentioned it to Miss Paul and her father the day they visited. Dr. Paul told me the last time he stopped by that Miss Shelley is moving to Bracebridge to be with her sister, and that her home would be available in two or three weeks. He thought we'd find it quite comfortable. It sounded very inviting, but I had to tell the doctor that until we'd actually sold the farm, we'd have no way of buying or even renting another place. Uncle Wesley's money will make things easier, but I need to be careful.

"Dr. Paul wants to be helpful, so he discussed the situation with Miss Shelley anyway. Now he's written with a very appealing offer."

Caleb breathed a big sigh of relief. Obviously, Dr. Paul had managed to convince Miss Shelley those rumours about his having been in jail were false. He was very grateful to the doctor for caring.

"There are about ten acres, so lots of room for you children to roam. There's also a barn for Bonnie, and room for the chickens and maybe even that calf Caleb is saving for. Miss Shelley's vegetable garden is well established, and she has a few apple trees as well. She's more interested in renting than selling, as she thinks she might one day return. She's offered it at a reasonable rate, but even a reasonable rate would not be easy for us to pay right now. It would work if we sold the farm quickly, but I don't know if we can expect to find a buyer fast enough."

Caleb happened to glance at Briar. She looked stricken, her eyes enormous. He caught his mother's eye and nodded in Briar's direction.

"What is it, Briar?" Mother asked. "Is something wrong?"

Lips trembling, Briar almost whispered, "Miss Shelley is a witch, and her house is haunted! Everyone says so. Oh please, Mother. Don't take us to a witch's house!" Tears filled her eyes.

"A witch?" Chantal gasped, terrified.

Mother looked astounded. "That's ridiculous. There's no such thing as a witch, Briar." Her voice became sharp. "Who's been saying this awful thing about poor Miss Shelley?"

Briar turned to Samantha, silently beseeching her help. After a moment, Samantha explained, "All the kids at school say she's a witch. She has a black cat, and . . . and . . . a snaggle tooth!"

"Oh, good heavens! Many people have black cats! And many people have crooked teeth. It doesn't make them witches! I told you, there's no such thing."

Samantha must have seen her mother was annoyed, but she couldn't resist adding, "Amy saw a ghost looking out a window one day, and she says

Miss Shelley makes secret teas and potions from the plants in her garden."

"Lord, give me strength!" their mother sighed. "Miss Shelley is a perfectly nice lady, and those children should be taken to task for telling such nasty lies! Now please—I would think my own children are too smart to believe such dreadful stories. You also know how much I hate gossip, and here you are repeating it."

The children sat very still and nothing more was said, but none of the girls looked convinced. Caleb thought, *More nasty rumours, but just kids saying crazy things about a poor old lady. Adults won't believe that, but some still might believe the lies about me.*

After a moment, Mother said, "Dr. Paul has made a suggestion. Miss Shelley is taking her cat with her to Bracebridge, but she can't take her beloved dog. If we offered to take good care of him and look after her garden, she would reduce the rate somewhat—"

"A dog!" Chantal's shriek of joy interrupted her mother.

"Calm down, dear," her mother admonished. "In addition, the Pauls are in need of a housekeeper a few days a week. They've asked if I might consider preparing some of their meals and doing some housework. It would mean a bit of income, of course, which we surely need. I think I'll go into town one day soon and look at Miss Shelley's cabin to make sure it's suitable for us."

"A dog!" Chantal repeated, unable to believe what she'd heard. 0Even though her mother had mentioned this idea of moving a few times in the past, it now seemed to be much more real and taking shape very quickly. Samantha felt she needed time to absorb it. What their mother was suggesting was a momentous change in their lives.

Leave the farm and move into town? She thought about the idea. Now that it was more of a reality than ever, she felt butterflies in her stomach. *This farm is the only home I know! It will all be so strange in town. What if I hate it? We probably couldn't come back.* She looked at her brother, trying to guess his thoughts.

***

Caleb closed his eyes to think over all that his mother had revealed about her plan. *I'm glad she's given up on the idea of Toronto. I know I was born there, but I don't remember anything about it! I'd probably hate it. It's been hard for her, and all of us, without Father. Everything's just harder without him, and everything she said in favour of moving into town sounds good.*

He opened his eyes to look at his mother and found she, in turn, was watching him. She seemed anxious to know his reaction to her news. *I guess it's because I'm the eldest*, he thought. *And I'm supposed to be the man of the house now.*

"I like the idea, Mother," he reassured her. "And I don't believe in haunted houses. I could still work for Mr. Whylie, and maybe I could find more work at one of the other farms closer to town as well."

Briar still looked unsure, but she put up a brave front. "I think I'd like living closer to school. But I'm glad Miss Shelley is taking that black cat with her!"

***

Samantha felt everyone's eyes on her. *What should I say? I like the idea of being closer to school and to most of my friends, but what if they keep on acting so strange? Maybe it wouldn't be so great.*

"Samantha, you seem worried, dear," her mother said.

I've got to say something. But what? Think fast! "It would be nice to have a dog!" she blurted out. "Even though it would really still belong to Miss Shelley; we could pretend it's ours. I wonder what its name is."

"But it would be our dog, wouldn't it, Mama?" Chantal asked. "We could call it Blackie."

"Blackie? Why Blackie?" Caleb laughed.

"Just because!" Chantal replied with indignation.

Mother looked relieved by their positive comments. "Nothing has been decided yet, but it does seem like an excellent opportunity."

I'm not so sure, Samantha thought.

"Are there any bears in town?" asked Chantal.

CHAPTER FORTY-ONE

A Visit to the Doctor's Office

A reluctant Andrew sat in Dr. Paul's office. This was not a good day. *Thanks to Caleb!* he thought. Even though a few days had passed since Caleb had come flying through the back door at the store and knocked him to the ground, Andrew was still experiencing more back spasms than usual, and the uncomfortable straight-backed chair he occupied wasn't helping. He crossed and uncrossed his legs, bounced his foot up and down, and shifted his position several times, all the while peering at the assortment of bottles lined up on a shelf across the room. Their mysterious contents and labels only added to his sense of foreboding.

Why was he here? He looked around Dr. Paul's office, a cozy room at the front of the house, simply furnished with an examining table, a vast desk piled with heavy books bearing medical titles, a worn brown leather chair behind it, and this one uncomfortable wooden one in front of it. On the wall hung a framed diploma and a photograph of a solemn-looking group of young men, presumably the doctor's medical school graduating class. Unfamiliar scents, not unpleasant but sharp and exotic, added to his sense of unease. Their source must be those mysterious bottles on the shelf.

That morning when he'd arrived to begin work, Mrs. Boyle had handed him a letter. "This is for you, Andrew. Someone slipped it under the door, either last night or very early this morning." Andrew was speechless; he had never received mail, and now he hesitated to take the envelope, almost as if he were afraid to touch something so rare. When he gave Mrs. Boyle an inquisitive look, she simply shrugged and looked away.

One word marked the front of the envelope: "Andrew." His hands shook as he tore it open to reveal a single stark line on an otherwise blank page: "Please come to my office when you have finished work." Below that line, he could just make out the scrawled signature: Dr. Paul. All day he had wondered and worried about the meaning of the note. By the time he arrived at the Pauls' house, he had worked himself up into quite a nervous state. When Heather Paul, beaming, greeted him at the door, he had embarrassed himself by stuttering something intended to be a polite response but sounding like gibberish. He couldn't remember exactly what he'd said, and now, sitting here thinking about it, he felt like an idiot. According to his daughter, Dr. Paul had been called away but would be back any minute. Andrew briefly considered slipping out before the doctor returned. That would only make him look more foolish, he decided, and besides, he needed to know why Dr. Paul had sent for him.

A grandfather clock in the hall ticked away the minutes. At last, Heather Paul appeared at the door to the little office and said, "I just saw Father's rig down the road. He'll only be a moment."

"Thank you," Andrew replied. He couldn't think of anything else to say.

She stood there for a moment, waiting for more, he supposed. "Well . . ." she said with a sigh, giving up, then turned and walked down the hall toward the kitchen. Andrew wished he could just disappear, but now he heard the clip-clop of Armon's hooves as the doctor pulled up in front of the house.

Too late. No way out now.

The sound of Dr. Paul's boots stamping the dust off on the porch mat was followed by the front door creaking open and the words "I'm home, Heather! Is Andrew here?"

"In your office, Father" came the reply from the kitchen. Andrew tensed. He stood as Dr. Paul, dusty, hot, and weary looking, entered the room.

"Afternoon, Andrew."

"Afternoon, sir."

"Sorry to make you wait. Mr. Barlow rode in to fetch me out to their farm. Young Bobby fell from the hayloft." Seeing Andrew's concerned look, he added, "He'll be fine. Just bruised and banged up a bit, nothing broken. He had a soft landing, thanks to some hay that happened to be in the right place."

"That's good." Andrew paused. "I got your note."

"Yes. Thank you for coming. I did want to speak with you in private. I'm glad to see you." The doctor walked behind his desk, put his black bag on the floor beside it, and sank into his leather chair. He stared at his folded hands resting on his lap. Andrew waited. Then Dr. Paul raised his eyes and looked at him. "How's your pain today, Andrew?"

"Not bad, sir," Andrew fibbed.

"Truthfully?" Andrew felt as if the doctor's eyes could see right through him and read his mind.

"Well, maybe a bit worse than usual," he answered, looking out the window. He didn't want to look at Dr. Paul. He felt as if he were being tested somehow. *What's he up to?*

"You remember I asked you once if you'd let me examine you—"

"I know," Andrew interrupted. "I don't want to be rude, sir, but nothing can be done."

"I'm not so sure," the doctor replied briskly. He leaned forward, resting his elbows on his desk, and studied Andrew's face. "I subscribe to some medical journals, Andrew. I like to keep up, and lately, there have been a couple of intriguing articles about back pain and helpful treatments. I also wrote to a former classmate who teaches at the university. He's been involved with a study that's provided some promising results in the short term and possibly long term as well. Not on every patient, you understand, but certainly a significant enough number to have attracted attention."

"Sir," Andrew shook his head." I told you before. I can't afford fancy treatments, especially if it means travelling to Toronto or somewhere, and I just don't want to get my hopes up and then find out I was right all along and nothing can be done. I couldn't take that. Thank you anyway, but I just can't. I'll manage as I am." He stood to leave and gasped as pain caught him halfway out of his chair, paralyzing him in an awkward position, his eyes squeezed shut and sweat forming on his brow. He felt the doctor's gentle hands on his shoulders. Something about this comforting gesture broke through Andrew's reserve; he heard a sob and realized it had come from him. Embarrassed, he brushed Dr. Paul's hands away. "Please," he whispered. "I need to go."

"You need to sit down for a minute—that's what you need to do. And listen. There's more I need to tell you. Hear me out, please." Taking care to prevent any abrupt movement that might bring on more pain, Dr. Paul eased him back into his chair. Andrew did not resist.

"Now," the doctor began, "there's a technique called subluxation, or manipulation of the spine. It's been used for centuries. Even the ancient Greeks knew about it and had some success treating back pain. They also used water therapy. You'd be surprised how advanced their knowledge was. Over the centuries, many different treatments have been tried, especially in times of war when men were often thrown from horses or even shot in the spine. Surgery was usually pretty crude on the battlefield or field hospitals, and about half the patients died, but even so, our knowledge of the human spine advanced little by little. My classmate at the university is using spinal manipulation and magnetic therapy. As I said, the results are promising, but there are no guarantees."

Andrew stared at his feet, listening but refusing to take any of these comments to heart.

Perhaps Doctor Paul could read his mind after all because he said, "I know you don't want to hear any of this. You've set your mind against it." He paused. "There would be no need to travel. I believe I understand enough to do the manipulation myself."

Andrew raised his eyes, something like hope stirring somewhere deep inside him. He tried to tamp it down, but the doctor quickly added,

"You have people who care about you, Andrew, believe it or not. Mr. and Mrs. Boyle called on me recently. They consider you a very valuable employee, and they've been doing some thinking about the future, yours and their own. They have no family, as you know, and they've been thinking of possibly turning the store over to you in a few years. You'd be partners to begin with, and you could slowly buy them out over time." He paused while Andrew absorbed this astounding news.

"But how? I mean, I can't do the heavy lifting or most of the other physical work," Andrew began. "It could never work. Besides, there's the farm. I was meant to be on the farm."

"There are always young people willing to do a bit of heavy lifting from time to time for some spending money," Dr. Paul said. "That doesn't need to be a problem. You have the brains for bookkeeping and stock-taking and running a business, young man, and this is an opportunity few are offered."

"But the treatments," Andrew said, returning to the original subject. "The cost..."

"As I said, you have friends. The Boyles have offered to help with fees, and I promise you, they won't be much. I'm anxious to hone my skills with this new treatment so that I might help others in future, and you would be helping me by allowing me to work on you. This arrangement, with luck, will help both of us. Again, there are no guarantees, but the outlook is promising."

Andrew's mind swirled with this unexpected turn of events. Dr. Paul gave him a moment to think before pressing his point. "If you'd do me the favour of allowing me to work on you, I'd like to start right away. How about coming back tomorrow after work?"

Dr. Paul's kind eyes were alight with excitement. Andrew could tell the man felt some confidence in what he was proposing. His own mind was full of conflicting emotions, and he looked away. There was so much to take in: the Boyles' incredible generosity, the doctor's enthusiasm for proceeding with this new treatment. *What was that word? Subluxation?* he recalled. *All it means is manipulation of the spine.* He was under no illusion such a procedure would be pain-free. The idea was frightening, there was no denying that. *But I have pain anyway. And maybe this pain would be worth it if I could feel some relief afterwards.* As if to confirm the point, another spasm seized his lower back.

When it had passed, he took a deep breath. *What have I got to lose?* Looking up at Dr. Paul, Andrew nodded his consent.

The doctor's face lit up, "Good man!" he exclaimed, clapping Andrew on the shoulder. "Good man! We'll start tomorrow! Now what do you say we go and see what my daughter has concocted for supper tonight?"

That was an offer Andrew could not resist. No need to deliberate; he accepted without a moment's hesitation.

***

In the village that night, neighbours stopped what they were doing as an unfamiliar sound caught their ears. Some were drawn to open their doors and step outside, so haunting was the sound. "Where's it coming from?" one called down the road to another.

"Sounds like the store!" came the shouted response.

The slightly hesitant playing of a waltz was followed by an attempt at a toe-tapping jig. "Someone's playing a fiddle!"

In their rooms above the store, Mr. and Mrs. Boyle were just getting ready for bed when the music began.

"It's coming from downstairs!" exclaimed Mr. Boyle. "What on earth's going on? I'd better have a look!" He prepared to go down and investigate.

"No, wait!" Mrs. Boyle put a hand out to stop him. "It's lovely, and I know who it is. Let him enjoy himself."

***

In his tiny room, Andrew's expression was pure delight as he lovingly drew the bow across the fiddle his mother had insisted he bring back to town with him. With each stroke his confidence grew. *Ma was right, he thought. I've missed this!*

Only later did he realize that, for a little while at least, he'd become so lost in his music, he'd been unaware of any pain in his body.

CHAPTER FORTY-TWO

The Storm

Thanksgiving Day arrived late on the calendar this year, and the weather had turned unseasonably hot again. Folks who kept a particularly sharp eye on the weather—most in a farming community—worried about how the hot spell would break. A slow cooling would be ideal, but if there was a sudden frost, the clash of hot air meeting cold could erupt into severe, possibly deadly storms.

However, after a mostly cool September, many were simply enjoying this unexpected and brief return of summer, especially the children playing at recess and after school. Most people took advantage of the opportunity to complete a few more outside chores. No one could predict how long this welcome warm spell would last.

Caleb laboured alongside Mr. Whylie, clearing more land of Muskoka's endless supply of rock and stones. He knew there wouldn't be much more outdoor work for him when the cold set in and winter approached. It could snow as early as four to six weeks from now. That was hard to believe when he was now sweating profusely.

I'm so thirsty, I could drink a gallon of water! Wouldn't mind some lunch either, but it's not even noon yet, he thought as he leaned on a spade. Straightening up, he looked over at Mr. Whylie. The older man seemed oblivious to the heat. *The minute he says we can take a break, I'm going to put my head under the pump and just get soaked!*

His glance strayed to the inviting water pump behind the house. May Whylie was sitting on the back stoop, and Charlie lay sleeping at her feet. May had missed school the past few days because of a worrisome, wheezing cough. Thankfully, this morning she was showing improvement, and with the weather so warm, her mother had instructed her to sit outside and soak up some sunshine. Mrs. Whylie believed that would be more beneficial than being cooped up in the house.

Without any warning, the day darkened ominously. Mr. Whylie scanned the sky. "Might have to pack it in soon. Looks like rain comin'. Maybe quite a storm. Look at those heavy clouds."

Caleb followed his gaze and nodded. "There's a change in the air, too. It feels strange." He noticed an odd silence. "Listen! Everything's so quiet. I can't hear any birds or crickets." Filled with a sense of foreboding, he asked, "Is everything covered that needs to be?"

"Should get the hay wagon into the barn. Some o' the last load is still sittin' on it. No sense lettin' that get soaked."

As if to make the point, a long menacing roll of thunder followed. Moments later, it was punctuated by a bang so loud, it must have made the windows rattle in the house. Caleb noticed the Whylies' dog scamper under the stoop where May had been sitting a few minutes earlier. *Poor thing sure hates thunder,* he thought.

As he and Mr. Whylie picked up their tools and raced toward cover, the farmer shouted, "No time to hitch up. You grab the front o' her to steer, and I'll push. The barn doors are open. We should get her inside in time."

Even with just half a load on the wagon, it was hard going, but they managed to roll the wagon in just as the heavens opened and the deluge began. Once the barn doors were shut, the two decided to wait it out inside the barn rather than try to make it across the yard to the house.

"These things pour heavy for a little while, then ease up pretty quick,"

Mr. Whylie observed. "Should ease up in about a quarter of an hour."

The storm had other ideas. It was as if a giant's knife had slashed a hole in the blue skies of heaven and all the rain that had ever been created poured straight down on that one farm. It bounced off the earth like rubber balls. Because the air had been so hot and the rain was so cool, a heavy fog slithered over the farm, coiling into every nook and cranny. It became impossible to see the house across the barnyard. In the barn, chickens squawked at the uproar, and the Whylies' horse banged about nervously in her stall.

"Wouldn't want to be caught out in this for long. It's about the worst I've seen in many a year," said Mr. Whylie. A few minutes later, after opening the door a crack to assess the situation, he turned back to Caleb with a worried frown. "At this rate, the creek's gonna rise really fast. Could be as bad as five years ago, when she flooded."

Caleb was alarmed. "Do you really think that could happen again?" He thought of his family. The girls should be in school, and surely Mother would be indoors. "If you're right, the roads might be washed out."

"Hard to say," Mr. Whylie's attention had wandered, as if he were trying to remember something important. Then it dawned on him. "I left that dang cow out in the field! I hope she stays there. Bossie's got a bad habit of wanderin' off in storms."

Several tense minutes later, although the rain still poured, it had eased up just enough that the two could see the house again. They decided to head for it. As they sloshed through thick mud and puddles, Mr. Whylie looked across the meadow for Bossie. She was not in sight. He called her name several times, but she didn't appear. Bossie could be finicky, but she usually responded when called.

"Dang! If she's wandered off again, she could be anywhere. Could be stuck in mud. Heaven help her if she's down at the creek. I suppose I'm gonna have to go lookin' for her."

"I'll help you," offered Caleb.

"Thanks. It can wait a little bit." They had reached the house. "Let's get inside for now and dry off some."

Soaked to the skin, they stepped in the back door, dripping pools of water. "I hope you've got the kettle on, Mother," Mr. Whylie called out amiably.

"We could both use a hot toddy."

His wife looked at the two of them and asked, "Where's May?"

"What do ya mean? She's here, isn't she?"

"No!" Mrs. Whylie was alarmed. "I thought she was in the barn with you!"

"I saw her sitting on the stoop just a little while ago," said Caleb.

"Oh, Jim! Where could she be? In this terrible storm . . ."

"Calm down now, Mother. Let me think for a minute." He took off his sodden hat, throwing more rain droplets around the room, and scratched his head, as if doing so might actually help him think better. "Bossie's wandered off again. You don't suppose May could've gone lookin' for her, do ya? And where's Charlie?"

"Charlie?" Mrs. Whylie looked momentarily confused. "I don't know. He must be with May. Oh, dear. She wouldn't be so foolish in all this rain, but the storm did come up very fast. Maybe she'd already started out, and she was caught in it. There's no shelter out there, and she's already sick with that cold. Oh, Jim!"

"Hold on! We'll head right back out and look for her. She can't be far. Bossie doesn't travel fast, if she's followin' that dang cow! Come on, Caleb!"

"Yes, sir!" Caleb was out the door before Mr. Whylie could even turn around and racing across the barnyard to the pasture. The mud really slowed him down, but he was still faster than the farmer. By the time he reached the pasture, he was so covered in muck that he almost looked as if he'd been dipped in chocolate.

"Head for the creek," Mr. Whylie shouted, as he huffed and puffed, trying to catch up.

Caleb took off as fast as the rain and mud would allow. The creek meandered through the farm, closer to the house and barn in some places than others. Here it was a good half mile across the field. As he ran, he called, "May!" several times, but there was no sign of the girl. He hoped he was heading in the right direction. She could have followed Bossie almost anywhere.

CHAPTER FORTY-THREE

Rough Water

The rain fell like a curtain, blinding Caleb. He realized that, without a visible landmark to orient himself, it would be easy to start moving in a wide circle without realizing it; inexperienced people lost in the woods often walked in circles. Forcing himself to concentrate on maintaining a straight line to the creek, he raced on.

He almost collapsed with relief when he found himself on the creek's bank. One moment he couldn't see anything, and the next, the swirling water appeared before him. Caleb paused, breathless; he leaned over, hands on his knees, sucking in gulps of air like a just-caught fish, and took in the frightening sight before him. What had been a quiet little stream was now raging and tossing, swollen with the rainfall. May was nowhere in sight.

Through thick bramble, he followed the creek for several hundred yards, peering into water and bush through veils of rain. Thorny branches caught at his sleeves and pant legs, slowing him down; a higher branch, which he'd pushed aside, snapped back in his face, missing an eye by a hair's breadth. Just ahead, in a slight clearing, Caleb spotted Bossie, her head hanging down, looking forlorn in the drizzle; when she recognized him, she bawled.

"Bossie, where's May?" Caleb called, feeling foolish even as he said it. *Do I actually expect her to answer?* The wet and muddy bovine bawled again.

As he approached Bossie, a flash of fur lunged at Caleb, almost knocking him flat. Charlie! The frantic animal howled and ran back and forth several times, as if heading off and then changing his mind. Each time he returned to Caleb, the dog barked, *He's trying to tell me something!*

"What is it, Charlie? Where's May?" Then Caleb realized the anxious creature was trying to lead him along the creek. "All right, boy, I'm coming. Where's May?"

Charlie turned in one swift motion and took off again. Caleb was right on his heels, but it was hard to keep up. Within seconds, the dog skidded to an abrupt halt and barked. Caleb scanned the area and spotted a flash of something blue at the water's edge. The colour was not natural; no plant he knew of was that particular shade. *May was wearing a blue dress today!* he recalled.

Racing forward, he caught sight of two legs trapped under a fallen tree. In a panic, he slipped down the muddy bank and into the raging water. May Whylie lay half in and half out of the swollen creek. Fortunately, her head was above water, but she was awfully still. "May!" he shouted. There was no response. Caleb was momentarily frozen in place. He didn't know what to think or do. *Oh, God, please don't let her be dead!*

Charlie continued his barking and pacing along the water's edge. All of a sudden, Mr. Whylie splashed into the creek and pushed past Caleb, yelling, "May!" He lifted his daughter's head and cradled it in his arms, saying her name over and over. There was still no response. "She's breathin'!" he yelled. "Help me get her out from under this tree."

Caleb prayed he had the strength to do what had to be done. The tree was not large—a medium-sized birch, and it had been dead for some time; the storm had simply helped bring it down. Like most dead birches, it was not as heavy as some other trees would have been, but lifting it was still a huge task for a fifteen-year-old boy. Mr. Whylie gently placed May down again and began to help push and drag the tree and all its branches off his daughter's lower limbs. As they strained to move it, the farmer slipped and went down hard. Suddenly, he was floundering under water. Caleb grabbed him and tried to help him back to his feet, but the man's shirt was tangled up in the leafy branches, and he couldn't stand up.

He spotted the knife Mr. Whylie carried in a leather pouch on his belt. Wrestling it out of the pouch, he slashed at the twisted shirt until it came free. In doing so, he managed to slash Mr. Whylie's arm as well, and blood trickled into the creek. The poor man leaned on Caleb as he tried to stand up. He was breathing hard and looked pale and dazed. Caleb helped him to the bank of the creek and sat him down. Then he turned back to the dead birch and pushed with every ounce of strength he possessed. The tree budged, but it wasn't quite enough. Assessing the situation, he realized he only needed to get a couple of smaller branches off May's legs. Grabbing the knife again, he began chopping and slicing at the branches furiously. At last, he had sliced through enough of them that he could break them off and release May's legs.

Mr. Whylie said in a raspy voice, "Thank you, boy. You've saved both of us today. Now, let's see if we can move her and get her home." He slipped back into the water and made his way over to May, calling her name again. This time, her eyes fluttered open for a minute and then closed again. A minute later, they opened again and she looked around, confused.

"Father?" May began to shiver violently and tried to sit up. With help from the two them, she managed it.

Charlie raced into the water and licked May's face over and over, as if she was the tastiest treat ever. It was enough to make her give a croaky laugh. "Oh, Charlie!"

Mr. Whylie yelled, "Get away, Charlie!" but the ecstatic animal kept on licking.

"May, how do ya feel? Do ya think you've broken anything? Can ya stand up? We've gotta get ya home." Her father's voice sounded strange, and Caleb was surprised to see tears in his eyes.

"I'm f-f-freezing and my h-head hurts," May said between teeth-chattering shivers. She must have seen the tears too, for she sounded alarmed when she added, "D-on't cry, Father! I'm sorry I went after B-Bossie."

"Never mind that, girl. The important thing now is to get ya home. The rest of it's all water under the bridge."

When Caleb realized what Mr. Whylie had just said, he chuckled; his relief at getting May and her father safely out of the creek was making him giddy.

May noticed him laughing, and her lips formed a wan smile. "W-water under the bridge!" she managed to repeat despite her exhaustion. "Father, you're f-funny!"

"Well, now I'm sure yer gonna be all right," her father declared. "If ya can make fun o' yer old man, yer just fine. Yer made o' good, tough stuff, just like yer ma."

With Caleb's and her father's help, May got to her feet, and it appeared she had no broken bones. Besides feeling frozen, all she had was a huge headache and some dizziness, she claimed. Although she insisted she could walk, her father insisted she be carried. Since he couldn't manage it with his injured arm, it was up to Caleb.

As Caleb scooped May up, he was surprised at how light she felt. She wrapped her arms around his neck and clung to him. Mr. Whylie, who had staunched his bleeding arm with his torn-up shirt sleeve, gave Bossie a good slap on her rump and told her to get along home. She seemed to listen and began trotting in the right direction, but he stayed right beside her just to be sure she made it back to the barn, and Charlie nipped at her heels for good measure. The worn-out group proceeded across the watery fields; they were muddy and soaked to the skin but joyful.

The rain had eased up but was still heavy. Mrs. Whylie, hair plastered to her head and soaked dress sticking to her small frame, ran and stumbled across the field to greet the exhausted rescuers and her daughter.

"Oh, thank you! Thank you! Thank you!" she kept repeating. It sounded like a prayer. When they came together, she took her daughter from Caleb, enveloped her in her arms, and hugged with all her might. She hugged as if she'd never, ever let go, but eventually she did, and then she hugged her husband. When she turned to Caleb, she didn't say a word, but he knew by the look in her eyes what she was thinking, and then she opened her arms once again and held him for a long time too.

As Caleb and a concerned Mr. Whylie watched, Mrs. Whylie seemed to gather herself together with a forced determination not to appear overly distressed or worried. She fooled no one.

"Now let's all have that hot toddy you asked for a while ago!" She smiled. "We'll need to draw a hot bath for May and get everyone into some dry clothes too."

Caleb and Mr. Whylie both smiled slightly when she added, "But Bossie, no hot toddy for you!"

CHAPTER FORTY-FOUR

Caleb's Challenge

In the Whylie kitchen, a full kettle of hot water was being kept warm on the back of the wood stove. "Good job I already had it boiling when you two came in from the barn!" Mrs. Whylie pointed out. "Jim, I need to get May and myself out of these wet clothes right away. You and Caleb should change too, but first let's get that hot toddy started. Do you remember how to do it?"

"What do ya mean, do I remember how to do it?" Mr. Whylie pretended to be indignant, but he winked at Caleb.

"Don't forget to add the honey," his wife reminded him as she and May disappeared behind the curtained entrance to a bedroom. A moment later, the curtain moved and her stern face peeked out. "And don't go overboard on the brandy!"

Caleb, trembling with cold, dropped onto a stool beside the warm stove. He didn't think his legs could take another step; he felt so tired. *If only I could crawl into bed now—I'd probably sleep forever.* His eyes felt heavier and heavier and began to close.

"Careful ya don't fall off that stool!" Caleb jerked upright. "Stove's mighty hot," Mr. Whylie warned. "You'd get a nasty burn for sure."

He watched the farmer pour hot water from the kettle into another pot, set it on a burner, pour in a generous amount of brandy, and drop in several spoonfuls of honey from a ceramic crock. As the man stirred, he occasionally brought the wooden spoon to his lips for a taste. "Ah, just what the doctor ordered!" he declared with a satisfied smile.

Caleb's shivering was abating as he warmed up beside the stove, but still, he reached out gratefully for the steaming mug Mr. Whylie handed him and took a gulp. The liquid seared his throat, which felt as if it might be on fire. Tears filled his eyes and ran down his cheeks. Then the choking began.

"Sip it, boy!" Mr. Whylie advised him. "Take yer time. There's alcohol in there, and I didn't stint on it, either."

"Y-y-yes, sir" was all Caleb could manage to get out. He wiped his eyes with a corner of his shirt and took a deep breath. When he felt ready to try the drink again, he took Mr. Whylie's advice to sip and felt the pleasant warmth of the soothing drink begin to seep through his body, relaxing him. A long-ago memory stirred. "I think my mother made this once, when I was little and got sick."

"Most likely," Mr. Whylie replied, smacking his lips. "It's good for what ails ya. Supposed to ward off colds. You got somethin' dry to put on?"

"Yes, sir. I'll do that right now." Caleb climbed to the small loft space where he slept whenever he stayed over and removed his filthy, sopping-wet clothes. Drying himself off with a rag, he slipped into dry pants and socks, and a warm shirt. The effects of the hot toddy and his fatigue overtook him, so he succumbed to an overwhelming desire to lie down on his mattress. In an instant, he was asleep.

***

The sound of anxious voices below woke Caleb. He looked around, confused. *Where am I?* his muddled brain wondered. *Who's that talking? Mother? No!* Raising himself up, he strained to listen.

"I tell you, I'm worried, Jim. She's so dizzy. Something isn't right!"

"I'm goin' for Dr. Paul—that's all there is to it! No point waitin' and wastin' time."

"Jim, we've never had a doctor come out. Can we afford it?"

"Maybe not, but we'll find a way. I'll get ready to go."

"But, Jim, your arm. It's not looking good, and the weather—"

"Hush now, Mother. You stay with May. I'll get my coat."

Caleb was alert now. He moved to the top of the ladder, poked his head out, and called down, "I'll go!"

Both Whylies looked up at him, surprised. Caleb scrambled down the ladder and jumped off the lower two steps, landing on his feet, as nimble as a cat. It was only then he noticed May, asleep on the old couch that had been moved closer to the stove. As she was wrapped in snug blankets, only her face could be seen; Caleb didn't think it was a good sign that she looked so pale.

"I said I'd go." Mr. Whylie's voice was firm.

"Jim, maybe you should let Caleb go . . . your arm . . ."

Before Mr. Whylie could object, Caleb said, "I'll be faster, and I know where he lives."

He saw Mr. Whylie hesitate. Before the man could speak, his wife rushed in and said, "Thank you, Caleb." She was visibly relieved. "I hate to send you out again in this weather. You've already done so much for us today." She looked away to hide her emotions.

"It's nothing." Caleb was embarrassed. "You've done an awful lot for me—and my family."

"Well, maybe I should stay here, just in case somethin' happens with May," Mr. Whylie said. "All right, boy, if it's all decided, you'd better take this heavy jacket o' mine." Grabbing a dark coat off a nearby peg, he held it out for Caleb to put his arms in. Caleb's shoulders sank under the weight of it.

"Thanks, but I think it would only slow me down," he said. Afraid he might have hurt the man's feelings, he attempted a joke. "I'd probably drown in a puddle!"

"Then take this." Mrs. Whylie went to a cupboard and took out a leather flask, which she filled with more hot toddy. Slinging the flask's long strap across his chest, Caleb grabbed his wretched, soaked boots. As he pulled them on over the dry socks he'd just changed into, he shivered and grimaced with disgust; the icy, cold boots felt slimy. Taking a deep breath, he opened the door and peered out; the miserable rain continued, although it was slowing down. He was reluctant to get soaked and chilled again, but he knew he had to go. *I've got to get to Dr. Paul's as fast as possible. May's life could depend on it!*

Mr. Whylie grabbed him by the shoulder and pulled him back. "Here—you can at least put this on yer head!" he insisted, planting a worn, wide-brimmed hat on Caleb's head. The thing slipped right down over his eyes. Pushing it farther back on his head, Caleb forced a smile and gave the Whylies a brief wave. Their worried faces seemed to focus all their hopes on him.

Oh, boy, he thought. *They're really counting on me. I'd better make it!* Feeling the weight of their expectations, he turned and stepped out into the rain. He felt very alone. *It's all up to me now.*

***

Caleb had only been on the road for ten minutes before he was soaked right through again. His clothes clung to his skin, and the rain had seeped through Mr. Whylie's hat. He'd seldom been so miserable, but he knew he couldn't take shelter, even if there was any to find. *I have to keep moving! I have to keep moving!* he kept thinking. Visions of May and Mr. Whylie trapped under the tree in the creek haunted him. The thought of May not recovering from her apparent head injury terrified him.

Deep mud slowed his progress and occasionally sucked a boot right off, forcing him to hop on one foot while he wrestled the boot free and fought to get it on again. One downed tree had already blocked his way, and he anticipated there'd be more. Its tangled branches made it impossible to climb over, so he'd had to detour through the woods for a stretch before finding the road again. All of this was making the journey twice as long as usual.

What if I can't even make it to town? What if it gets dark before Dr.

Paul can make it back to the farm? What if he isn't home? All these dark what-ifs swirled through his mind, like mud swirling through the creek.

Caleb uncorked the flask slung over his shoulder, and remembering to sip this time, drank a little of Mr. Whylie's hot toddy. *Got to make this last; there's a long way to go yet. . . if I can get through.* He was more concerned than ever about getting through now that the road was becoming impassable. No one else was out and about. *It's as if I'm the only living creature on the face of the earth,* he thought, and a depressing feeling of loneliness filled him. All of a sudden, an image of the enormous moose he'd come face to face with on his journey home popped into his head, and he stopped to peer at his surroundings. Not only did he feel lonely but also nervous. *Of all people, I should know you're never really alone out here!* Then he thought, *But surely not even a moose would be dumb enough to wander around in this storm . . . would it?*

***

By the time town came into view, Caleb was in a stupor, barely thinking, just putting one foot in front of the other. *Shanks mare,* he remembered. *Just put one foot in front of the other.* Dragging himself up the steps at Dr. Paul's house, he knocked once on the door, then sagged against it, waiting and listening for the sound of approaching footsteps; there was only silence. *No one's home!* His disappointment was so intense, he slid down to the porch floor, defeated. *Where could they be? They can't be out in this storm! What'll I do next?* Desperate, he lifted an arm, pounded on the door several times with all the force left in his body, and pressed an ear to the door to listen. *Please, let him be home!*

CHAPTER FORTY-FIVE

Storm's Aftermath

Andrew perched on an uncomfortable stool beside the old couch where May still slept. His heart was nearly broken at the sight of her bruises and the thought that he'd almost lost her. He was still in a state of deep shock.

It was only a few hours since an anxious Dr. Paul had stopped at the store to pick him up. Listening to the doctor explain the desperate circumstances to Andrew, Mrs. Boyle had immediately cried, "Drop everything and go!" And he had.

Dr. Paul had left Caleb asleep under a stack of warm blankets on a couch in his living room and fervently hoped Armon could get his buggy through to the farm. The storm had passed, but there was flooding in some low places, and the roads were a muddy mess. He warned Andrew that if they had to abandon the buggy and walk, they would.

They moved painfully slowly. Andrew struggled to hide his impatience. *Even I could have walked faster than this!* he kept thinking. He peppered Dr. Paul with questions about May, trying to understand how such a terrible event could have happened.

"I'm afraid I just don't have any answers for you," the doctor told him. "Like I said at the store, Caleb was too exhausted to give me details. All I know is there was an accident at the creek, but May is home and in bed now. Your parents must be very worried though, to send for me."

This response didn't reassure Andrew at all, but it seemed to be all he was going to get. Dr. Paul seemed lost in thought for a while. When he spoke again, there was admiration in his voice. "Somehow young Caleb managed to trudge all the way to town in that deluge. It must have been too risky to try your father's horse and wagon, and even Caleb barely made it through on foot. He's made of strong stuff, that one."

Those words of praise hadn't improved Andrew's mood. Now, in the warmth of his mother's kitchen, he realized how lucky they'd all been. Dr. Paul had insisted on making a quick stop at the school to make sure his daughter and the children were all right. It was after six o'clock, and even though he was impatient to get home, Andrew agreed this had to be done. Besides, part of him wanted to see the teacher again. Dr. Paul interrupted Andrew's thoughts. "I hope none of the children got caught in this storm."

Heather Paul had been sufficiently concerned about flooding that she'd wisely kept the children at school until the worst of the torrential rain had passed. As soon as it began to ease up, several parents arrived to gather up the children and see them safely home. The last were just leaving.

"They weren't frightened," she told her father. "In fact, most of them thought having to wait out the storm was a great adventure! And there's no need to worry about me," she rushed to add, noting his concerned look. "I won't have any problem getting home now. You need to get going and see to poor May."

"Well, you be careful," her father replied. "There's a lot of mud and huge puddles out there." He smiled. "You don't want to disappear in one of them!" Then he became more serious. "I likely won't make it back tonight. If you need anything, go to Mrs. Boyle."

"Of course," Miss Paul replied. Then she turned to Andrew. "I'm so sorry. I hope May will be all right. I'm glad you're going to be with her and your parents. You'll be a comfort to them." Andrew nodded his thanks. He was so anxious to get home now that they knew all was well at the school, he couldn't think about anything else.

"Hurry!" Miss Paul urged her father. "May needs you."

***

When the doctor and Andrew made it through to the farm at last, they found that Mrs. Whylie had bathed her shivering daughter in a hot bath, then wrapped her up in comforters, wisely laying stones she'd warmed in the oven under the covers. She had cleaned and expertly wrapped her husband's wound, and he sat on a rocking chair pulled up close beside his daughter. Charlie helped him stand guard; the dog hadn't left May's side. As Andrew petted Charlie and ruffled his fur, he thought how strange it seemed to see May dozing on the old couch where their father often took a nap after lunch.

Dr. Paul woke May for his examination and later declared her to be in fairly satisfactory shape, all things considered. "But she's going to need at least another week of rest. Maybe keep her on fluids for a couple of days. We don't want to bring on any vomiting." He also declared Mr. Whylie's wound very well cleaned and tended to by Mrs. Whylie, whom he insisted would make an excellent nurse. May and Andrew had never seen their mother blush before, but she certainly had at the doctor's compliment.

"You're not going to set out for home now, are you, Doctor? It'll soon be dark, you can't trust the roads. And you'll have missed your dinner too. You'll stay and have a bite with us, I hope."

"Thank you kindly, Mrs. Whylie. I think I'll stay at least till first light. I can sit with May through the night and keep a close eye on her. She's going to be fine, but I'd rest easier if I stayed."

"Thank you, Doctor. We're most appreciative." She busied herself at the stove, swinging its big door open and throwing in more wood.

Dr. Paul sighed and rubbed his eyes as he took a seat at the table. It had been a long day, and he was tired. For a moment, he seemed lost in thought. Then he spoke in a soft, weary voice. "Thank God young Caleb was there to help. Things might not have turned out so well if he hadn't been."

"Yes," agreed Mrs. Whylie. "We owe him a great deal. I can't bear to think what might have happened to May without his quick actions. He saved Jim too."

"That he did," said her husband. "He's a brave young man."

As Andrew listened to his parents and Dr. Paul, that part of him that seethed with jealousy toward Caleb wanted to scream in anger against their good words. Releasing May's hand, he stood with difficulty, ignoring his body's strong protests. Being bounced around in Dr. Paul's buggy on what was left of the rough roads after the storm had been a new form of torture. Andrew made his way over to the window and watched the dying daylight sparkle and dance in the remaining puddles.

He pressed both hands to his mouth, as if to hold in the angry words that threatened to erupt.

Deep down, he knew Dr. Paul and his parents were right. If it weren't for Caleb, he might well have lost his sister, and his father too. But it was a bitter pill to swallow. Andrew's emotions struggled against each other: the old jealousy and anger up against relief and gratitude. When he thought of how badly he'd treated the boy, and the rumour he'd started, a different emotion arose, taking him by surprise: he felt deeply ashamed.

He felt his mother's eyes on his back; it was funny how she could do that, make him feel as if she could read his mind. He knew she wasn't going to let him off easily.

"Andrew? A penny for your thoughts."

He turned to face her. From a long-dead place deep within, he dragged up the difficult words. "Oh, I was just thinking, like you, Ma, that Caleb was very brave, and we really should be grateful. It's good that Father has him helping around here." He slumped back into the chair beside May, as exhausted as if he were at the end of a long-fought battle.

"Amen to that!" said his mother with a weary smile.

***

Andrew chose his moment with care. He waited until Mr. Boyle was nearby, then took his pencil out of his pocket, as if to make a note. Pretending to be clumsy, he dropped it and watched it roll away. *Not quite the right spot, but close.*

"Oops! I'll get it," he said to Mr. Boyle. Bending over, he stopped halfway, pretending his back had seized up again. As he straightened up, he allowed his toe to kick the pencil into place.

"Here, I'll get it," Mr. Boyle offered. "You watch that back of yours."

"Thank you, sir." Andrew watched as the older man struggled to get down on his knees and peer under the table where the pencil had rolled.

With one arm extended, Mr. Boyle felt around until he latched onto something. Then his face took on a puzzled look. "What's this?" he asked as he withdrew his arm.

Yes! Andrew smiled to himself as he helped his boss struggle to his feet. *It was a pretty good plan after all. No one will ever be the wiser.*

"Well, I'll be darned!" Mr. Boyle muttered.

"What is it?" his wife asked absentmindedly. She was intent on catching a stitch that had slipped in her knitting.

"Look! It's the knife! The one that's been missing."

"Well, will wonders never cease! Where'd you find it?"

"It was just under this table. If we hadn't been looking for the pencil Andrew dropped, I'd never have spotted it. The pencil rolled under the cabinet, and there was the knife!"

"It's funny you didn't find it earlier when you swept the floor. I always said you do a half-hearted job of it!"

Mr. Boyle was indignant at the accusation. "There's nothing wrong with my sweeping! And I swear I searched this area thoroughly when it went missing all that time ago!"

"Well, just be glad you didn't accuse Caleb of taking it. That would have been dreadful."

"You're right," her husband conceded. Then, with an impish grin, he added, "For once!"

Andrew smiled. He felt good—much better than he had in a very long time.

CHAPTER FORTY-SIX

Saying Goodbye

Samantha loved October. For her, it was one of the most breathtakingly beautiful months on the farm. With the breaking of the earlier heat wave, frosty nights had set to work painting nature's brilliant reds and golds to dance and dazzle in the crisp sunshine.

After the fierce rainstorm, a string of golden days had lifted the spirits; today, however, Mother Nature couldn't seem to make up her mind about the weather. Samantha noticed that this uncertainty matched her own mood. Either the sun popped out with an uplifting warmth or disappeared behind banks of dark, threatening clouds. In turn, she was alternately elated by her family's new adventure of moving into town or sad at leaving this special piece of earth, the only home she'd ever known in her young life.

She noticed that Briar and Chantal too were either laughing and teasing each other one moment or being quiet and thoughtful the next. They understood well the magnitude of the change they were embarking on, and although they seemed excited about it, Samantha knew from whispered conversations at bedtime that they were also nervous about leaving the familiar for the unknown. She sensed that Caleb shared their mood today.

***

Taking a pause from loading Mr. Whylie's buckboard, Caleb observed his mother and sisters. He wasn't as conflicted as they were about moving. *It's the right decision. I know it! Even though we don't know how things are going to go in town, staying here would just get harder every year. At least now there's a chance things will look up.*

In the bone-chilling dampness of early morning, he had huddled with his mother and sisters beside the graves of his father and the two infant brothers he had never really known. With the sweet morning songs of forest birds as accompaniment, they had spoken their words of farewell, the most wrenching part of this leave-taking for everyone.

In contrast, the sweetest part for Caleb was when his mother had said, "Caleb, we could never have left here not knowing where you were. I'm so thankful you're back and we can make a fresh start together, as a family."

Like a mother hen with her brood of chicks all cozily nestled under her wings, his mother could settle contentedly at last. Once the decision had been made to move, she appeared to have never second-guessed herself. *Until today, perhaps,* Caleb thought.

He had observed her as they packed up of their few belongings and emptied the cabin. He knew she felt saddened, perhaps more than she'd expected, and he could tell by her forced cheerfulness that she was trying hard to hide these emotions from her children.

Caleb thought that seeing the meagre possessions accumulated from all those backbreaking years on the farm must have been a sharp reminder to his mother of how desperate their situation had become. In the face of all this, she seemed determined to be positive and to look forward to her new home and life in the village.

His mother would be working at the Pauls' home a few hours a week and might find some sewing as well; she'd also continue selling eggs and preserves. He would carry on working two days a week at the Whylie farm and had let other farmers know he was available. He might not find additional work until spring, but he was optimistic. If necessary, he'd apply to the lumber camp near Baysville for winter work. He thought of his old friends who had moved on to other places and other jobs. *Maybe someday I'll get a chance to be a smithy like Peter. Living in town, I might hear of more opportunities.*

In the past few months, Caleb had heard stories from the Whylies about some other struggling farmers in the area who had been forced to abandon their farms. Thinking about these sad tales, he'd been struck by a clear realization: *Even if I hadn't run away, my family would still be in big trouble. The farm's been draining us all for years, and Father's death just made matters worse. It isn't all my fault just because I left!*

His relief was immense, and as uncertain as the future might look for his family right now, he also felt proud about the money he had saved to buy a calf one day. *Even if I don't ever spend it on that calf, it's going be a big help.*

Naturally, he experienced a tug in his heart for this home his family had carved out of the forest, and he would never forget the adventures they had shared here. He let his gaze wander over the sun-dappled little clearing, with the cabin he could remember his father building and the vegetable garden his mother had planted and treasured. At that moment, under the October sun, it looked idyllic, and he almost had second thoughts about leaving. *But,* he reminded himself with a smile, *this isn't goodbye just yet. I'll come back from time to time to keep an eye on things until it's sold.*

He returned to the job at hand, stacking the mahogany dining chairs securely in the wagon. The drive into the village would take at least two hours. Glancing at Briar and Chantal, he thought, *With luck, they'll sleep most of the way.*

Briar looked up and smiled when she saw Caleb watching. Only he knew her little secret. When no one else was looking, she had revealed to her big brother a tiny bundle, wrapped in a scrap of cloth and hidden in her pocket.

"May Whylie told me if I sprinkle salt in front of Miss Shelley's door, it will ward off evil witches!" she'd announced in all seriousness. This was news to Caleb, but he knew better than to make fun of the idea.

"Well," he'd replied, choosing his words with care, "May usually knows what she's talking about." *It's not a lie,* he reasoned. *She usually does, but not this time!*

***

The moment finally arrived when there was nothing left to do. Everyone was either in the buggy or on the cart ready to depart, except for Caleb's mother. Her children watched as she entered the cabin one last time. They could just see her standing quietly inside the door. She lifted her head and turned in a slow circle, closing her eyes briefly, as if she were breathing in the familiar scents and memories of the empty cabin one last time. Then, with a brave smile for them, she came back outside, gently closing the door behind her.

Mr. Whylie gave his horse a "Giddy-up!" and with a sudden lurch, the wagon moved forward. Behind him, Caleb heard Dr. Paul flick his buggy's reins and Armon's nickering as he began to pull. The wheels of the heavily laden buggy creaked. As the wagon bounced and jerked, Caleb held on tight to his seat. He felt a surprising lightness in his heart, as if a burden had been lifted and a great adventure was beginning.

Chantal, suddenly awake and lively, shouted, "Bye, house! Bye!" Briar laughed and repeated it.

Caleb and Samantha looked at each other and grinned, then the two of them called out, "Bye, house."

Turning around to watch his mother in Dr. Paul's buggy, Caleb hoped she'd add her own light-hearted "Goodbye, house!" and join in the playful spirit Chantal and Briar had shown. It would be as if she were giving her blessing to their old home and to their new life at the same time.

But his mother's head was bowed, and Caleb couldn't see her face. He felt a sense of disappointment. *I guess she's sad,* he thought. Then she did turn to look back over her shoulder at the house. When she turned forward again, she saw him watching and gave him a wave and a bright smile. She straightened her spine so she sat erect, chin up, giving her face a determined look as if she was facing her future with confidence. Her lips were moving, and although the creaking wagon made it impossible to hear, Caleb was certain she was saying, "Goodbye, house."

He felt hopeful, but deep down he also understood he had little control over what the future might hold. All he could do was his best. Would that be enough? *I sure hope so!*

CHAPTER FORTY-SEVEN

Haunted House

Once on their way, the drive to the village became an adventure. Bumpy roads did their best to upset stomachs and dislodge parcels, but Caleb was pleased that everything and everyone seemed well secured. Brilliant red and gold leaves stirred in the trees, delighting the eye. Even the road appeared festive, adorned with those leaves the autumn wind had dislodged from their branches. Eventually, the bouncing wagon and buggy lulled his sisters, curled up under layers of cozy quilts, to sleep. He and the adults remained alert, however, as axles creaked, protesting their load.

His mind wouldn't let him rest and be happy for long, so all the possible problems he anticipated began to turn over and over in his brain. *Will we really be better off in the village? What if I can't find enough work to help keep us going? I sure hope someone buys the farm. The sooner the better!*

***

The horses' slowing pace woke Samantha. Eager anticipation and nervous trepidation rumbled together in her tummy, and she craned her neck for a good look as Miss Shelley's house came into sight. This impressive cabin dwarfed the one her family had just left, and even so late in the year, a few shocks of happy colour brightened the garden. Glass windows so clean they sparkled in the afternoon sun dazzled the eye.

Pulling up to a stop in front of the house, the family regarded their new home for a quiet moment before stretching their stiff limbs and gingerly climbing down from their perches.

The front door opened with a creak, and all heads turned toward it. A tiny lady with a crown of snow-white hair came toward them. Her black dress stood in stark contrast to her hair.

"Welcome!" she called in a cheerful voice. "My goodness, you've made good time!"

"Good afternoon, Miss Shelley," said Dr. Paul. "Yes, we're all here, safe and sound." He climbed down from his buggy and offered his hand to help Mother down.

"Miss Shelley. How lovely to see you again," Mother said.

"Well, I did say I'd be here to see you safely ensconced in your new home and make sure you know your way around."

"Miss Shelley sounds like a normal person," Briar whispered. *Was her sister starting to have doubts?* Samantha wondered. Then Briar added, "But maybe witches can do that. We'll have to be careful. She fooled Mother and Dr. Paul, but she can't fool me!"

Samantha wasn't so sure. It occurred to her that Miss Shelley was probably exactly what Mother said she was, a perfectly nice old lady. Still, she would have to stay on her toes, just in case.

Just then, their mother called to them to come and meet the woman. Nodding to Briar, Samantha said, "I guess we should go and find out for ourselves." Taking Chantal by the hand, she moved closer.

While they were being introduced, the three solemn little girls couldn't take their eyes off Miss Shelley's unfortunate front tooth.

A gnarled hand reached out to grab Samantha's and shook it. "I'm so pleased to meet you, Samantha."

Samantha was about to wipe her hand on her dress when she stopped herself. You could get warts from witches, according to her friends, but if Miss Shelley was just a nice old lady with a sweet face, as she was now prepared to believe, then wiping her hands would be rude.

"I hope you'll enjoy living in this house," Miss Shelley continued. "Most importantly, I hope you'll take good care of Rascal for me."

"Rascal?"

"Rascal is my dog. He's half deaf or he would have been here to meet you by now. He'll show up any minute, I'm sure."

As if on cue, an old brown-and-grey dog loped across a field, tail wagging, and stopped at Samantha's feet. Drool slid from a corner of his mouth. Excitement danced in his eyes.

"Look at his eyes!" Briar exclaimed, laughing. "They're different colours."

"Oh, my goodness! One is light blue, and the other one is . . . yellow," said Samantha with a giggle.

"He has a crooked tail," Chantal added. "It's all curly."

"Rascal is probably part Husky," Miss Shelley explained. "With that curl at the tip of his tail and his one light blue eye, that would be my best guess. I regret I can't take him with me to Bracebridge. He's been a marvellous companion for many years. But as he's getting old, it will be nice for him to remain here in familiar surroundings. I'll come back some time to visit him, and I'll tell you all about what he likes to eat and what some of his favourite things are. Your mother has assured me you'll all be kind to him."

"Oh, we will. We will!" Briar and Chantal were already dancing around Rascal, patting his head and tickling him behind his pointy ears. Samantha loved the feel of the dog's sleek fur coat. She thought she could just stand there all day, running her hands through it. However, as much as Rascal enjoyed being stroked, he was a dog made for playing, and if dogs could smile, he did. Circling, jumping, lunging, and intent on fun, he led the girls across the garden and into a field.

"I can see that Rascal is going to be just fine." Miss Shelley smiled. "Now I've boiled the kettle, so please do come in for a cup of tea before unloading. You must be chilly."

Caleb turned from watching his sisters playing with Rascal to regarding his mother, as if he were trying to read her face. She smiled, and a tiny tear slipped down her cheek. "It's good to be here at last," she said, slipping her arm through his. "Now come and see our new home."

***

That night Caleb lay awake for a while adjusting to the strangeness of the new house. His body was tired, but his mind was busy. *I can't believe we're really here! It feels good, like things are going to work out after all. And the girls have stopped talking about witches at last. Don't think I could have taken much more of that.*

A soft groan caught his attention. Through his open door, he watched as Rascal flopped down and settled outside the bedrooms, content to be near everyone. Soon Caleb could tell by the animal's breathing that he was asleep. He didn't seem to have realized yet that Miss Shelley would not be returning for a long time, if ever. He was just a dog doing what dogs do best, guarding his friends and dreaming of chasing squirrels. Sometimes his paws moved in his sleep and he made little yipping sounds. *Those squirrels must be leading him on a merry chase,* thought Caleb. Then he drifted off to sleep himself, putting his worries out of mind for the time being.

CHAPTER FORTY-EIGHT

The Party

"Samantha, how would you like to have a party?"

"A party?" Samantha was surprised at her mother's question.

"Yes, to celebrate our new home. I thought you girls might invite your friends to tea. I could make cranberry scones if you like, and maybe an apple pie." Mother was enthusiastic. "You could play some games. Maybe bob for apples."

Samantha didn't seem to know how to respond. Caleb was as surprised as his sister at this unexpected suggestion. He knew his sister's friends still teased her about living in a haunted house, and he could almost read her mind: *What if I invite them and they won't come?*

Mother also noticed her hesitation. "Don't you like the idea, Samantha?"

"Oh, I do, I do!" Still, she hesitated.

"But?" Mother's eyes searched her face for a clue.

"Well, it's just that I don't know if anyone would come," she blurted out, confirming Caleb's suspicions. "They still talk as if it's a haunted house."

"Then here's a perfect opportunity to demonstrate it isn't."

Caleb gave Samantha a sympathetic look. It wasn't easy to win an argument with Mother.

***

The next day, Samantha and Briar approached their friends at recess. It was almost November, and the wind carried a nip of winter. The girls huddled in a corner for shelter, stamping their feet and blowing on their fingers to keep warm. They looked miserable.

"Maybe this isn't such a good idea," Samantha whispered to Briar.

"I know, but we don't really have a choice," her sister replied. "Mother will want to know how it went."

"Right. Well, here goes, then."

Arlene looked up and smirked. "How's the ghost? Keeping you up at night?"

"I could never sleep in that house!" Amy added.

"There never was a ghost," Samantha countered. "And Miss Shelley is just a nice old lady, not a witch."

"So you say," Victoria chimed in. "My sister says different. She got a magic love potion from her, and it worked. She's getting married."

"You told us that before," Briar said. "Maybe she was just going to get married anyway. Did you ever think of that?"

Before things deteriorated any more, Samantha thought she'd better extend the invitation—but she was sure she'd only be further humiliated.

"We're going to have a party. You're invited, if you're not all too scared to come." She was aware of the challenge in her voice. *So it wasn't a very graceful invitation!* she thought. *I'm not sure I really want them to come anyway.*

"What kind of a party?" Victoria was obviously intrigued. "When?"

"Sunday afternoon. It's to celebrate our new home. My mother is going to do some special baking and make a fancy tea. We could play some games too." She could see she had piqued their interest, as they all shifted their eyes to glance at each other, assessing what their reactions should be.

"I'll have to ask my mother if I'm allowed," Arlene said.

"Me too," echoed Amy.

Victoria remained quiet, apparently waiting to see what the other two decided.

"That's fine. Suit yourselves. Chantal is going to invite Tara, and we've already invited May. The party is definitely on, so just let us know if you're able to come. Or if you'd rather, I guess our mother could speak to your mothers..."

"No, that's all right," Arlene said quickly. "We'll let you know tomorrow." Then she added a rather late, "Thank you."

Miss Paul shook her handbell. Recess was over, and everyone hurried to the warmth inside.

***

Sunday afternoon, Samantha helped her mother lay out her best tablecloth and china teacups and saucers, just as they had when Miss Paul came to tea. Their mother's efforts to make the day special were beyond expectations, and the girls couldn't wait for their friends to arrive, though they still didn't know quite how some of them would react to being in "the witch's haunted house." Caleb was driving May in from the farm. The other girls would walk over.

Samantha hugged her mother. "I can't believe you're letting us use your good dishes. Thank you so much. I just hope my friends don't spoil things. They really surprised me when they said they'd actually like to come."

"Well, I wasn't quite as surprised as you, dear. Curiosity is a powerful motivator. I imagine they're just dying to see what it's like in here, and their curiosity won out over their fear. They were just being silly anyway. They probably know that."

"I hope so," Samantha said. "Remember that saying? 'Curiosity killed the cat.' I guess it's curiosity that made them say yes."

The sound of girls' chatter floated through the windowpanes. Samantha opened the door to the chilly wind and ushered her friends inside. They were quiet upon entering but remembered their manners and said hello to her mother.

"Please have a seat at the table," Mother said. "I hope you girls all like cranberry scones and apple pie."

"Oh, yes, ma'am!"

As the guests took their places, their eyes widened at the beautiful china and tablecloth. "My, this is pretty," Amy said. "I've never seen such beautiful dishes."

"Thank you, Amy. Since this is a tea party and you're all becoming such young ladies, I thought they suited the occasion."

"Thank you," replied Victoria, blushing.

Arlene looked embarrassed. "Yes, thank you, Mrs. Lawson."

Mother busied herself with the kettle, and the girls sat around the table, mostly looking at their hands. They didn't seem to know what to say.

Before things became too awkward, Caleb pulled up with May in the wagon, and the two of them came chattering and laughing into the room. With Caleb's good humour and teasing, the other girls relaxed, and the party began.

He even made a few jokes about the ghost. "It's very good-natured and helpful. Sometimes when I'm home it makes my bed. It's like having my very own servant! I'm glad Miss Shelley left him behind. Or her!"

The girls made a big to-do about not believing him, of course, so he persisted with his comical ghost stories.

"I'm not kidding. Some mornings it even brings me tea in bed, but it never stays to have a cup with me. I wonder, do ghosts leak if they drink? Would the tea run out all over the floor?"

Samantha watched Caleb with gratitude and admiration. He knew just how to ease a situation. He reminded her of their father long ago. Maybe life in the village was going to work out after all. Observing her friends listening to her brother, she realized he had probably also won a few hearts. She wondered if he was even aware of that fact. When he smiled at her, she rewarded him with a huge grin and thought once again how thankful she was he had come home.

CHAPTER FORTY-NINE

Christmas Eve

The children's mother often spoke of the September day when Dr. Paul had picked her up in his buggy and brought her to see Miss Shelley's cabin for the first time. "I'm eternally grateful," she would say. "I knew immediately this would be a perfect home for us."

Originally built for a larger family, it was so much more spacious than their cabin, and with other pleasing features. No one had to climb a ladder to sleep in the loft, for example, as there were enough rooms on the main floor. The barn was in good shape, and the vegetable garden was a dream come true for Mother. There was even a well! "We don't have to carry water from a stream!" Samantha had exclaimed. Although the idea of having neighbours so close by was going to take some getting used to, it was really a good thing for many reasons, including emergencies.

Once their mother had made the necessary arrangements with Miss Shelley and put the farm up for sale, the little family had closed one chapter in their lives and opened another. The closed chapter had been important for the

Lawson children: homesteading with their parents and the family life they'd enjoyed together while their father was still alive. They would never forget a moment of it.

Now they were settled in Miss Shelley's comfortable house, enjoying the new chapter and very glad of the decision their mother had made. The arrival of Uncle Wesley's generous cheque had been a blessing and would make life much easier for a while. Caleb knew, however, that their financial future was still a little uncertain. *At least until a buyer for the farm comes along,* he thought, but he was trying hard not to worry.

Mother kept saying how proud she was of her children, "You've all been wonderful. I'm so pleased at the easy adjustment you seem to be making to living in town." She was also exceedingly thankful for the Pauls' friendship and kindness, and not just because Dr. Paul had found this new home for her family. Seeing their mother more relaxed and less worried made her children more relaxed and happy too.

***

Christmas Eve! It's finally here! Samantha, her face glowing from the brisk air, rushed in from the barn, where she had just taken a special treat to Bonnie in her new stable. Miss Shelley's dog followed her like a shadow. Rascal was a very loveable but odd-looking dog. With his light brown coat mottled with grey and his tail curled at the tip, he did remind people of a Husky, just as Miss Shelley had said. But it was his startling, mismatched eyes that really caught their attention. The poor thing had missed Miss Shelley so much at first that he had stopped eating, but with a great deal of love and attention, he gradually became part of the Lawson family. Now Rascal felt it his duty to guard them at all times, which was why he'd accompanied Samantha to the barn. He'd even become used to Bonnie and was often found curled up in her stall, enjoying a visit.

As she entered the large cabin, Samantha smiled at her mother, thinking as she often did how glad she was they had decided to move here. She had loved the farm, but she truly enjoyed living closer to other families and to school. Sometimes she stayed after school, helping Miss Paul. Her teacher understood Samantha's longing to be a teacher one day too and encouraged her in her dream. Samantha was beginning to believe that dream might come true one day.

Even Amy, Arlene, and Victoria didn't seem to be acting quite so prissy anymore. She didn't understand why, but it was fine with her. They no longer teased her about being a tomboy, and she was sure they now felt very foolish about insisting Miss Shelley was a witch. She remembered how Briar had secretly sprinkled a tiny amount of salt in front of all the doors on moving day. It had helped her feel better, and Samantha would keep her sister's secret forever.

She inhaled the fresh pine fragrance of the tree standing in a corner. "Is it time to decorate the Christmas tree yet?"

"As soon as your brother arrives. He shouldn't be long now."

Briar and Chantal entered the room carrying a long chain made of links of paper. "Do you think we've made it long enough?" Briar asked.

"I think so, dear. It's a small tree. We can start popping some corn now to string into another garland."

December 24th was also Briar's ninth birthday, and between celebrating her sister's birthday and waiting for Christmas, Chantal was actually dancing and jumping around with excitement. "Can we eat some of the popcorn? Does it all have to go on the tree? When will we have the birthday cake?"

"Oh, Chantal!" laughed Briar. "You really are a little rascal."

"No-o-o, Rascal is a dog!" Chantal giggled.

Mother laughed aloud. "You two are funny!" Then she added, "It makes me so happy to see all of you happy too."

***

As Caleb walked home from the Whylies' farm, he was glad the wind had dropped. The afternoon was cold and nippy enough without any strong gusts adding to the chill. His snowshoes crunched through the top layer of snow but kept him from sinking much farther into it. He could feel his fingers and toes becoming numb and would have shoved his hands in his pockets for warmth if he hadn't needed to keep his arms free to maintain his balance on the snowshoes.

The Whylies would be joining his family later in the afternoon for the Christmas and birthday celebrations. Caleb could have come in the wagon with them then, but once his work was done he was anxious to leave earlier. *Besides, I like this walk. Gives me time alone to think.*

His thoughts tonight were of the past six months since his homecoming. So much had happened in such a short period that it made his head spin. So much had been difficult, but in the end, much had made him feel good about returning. That he'd arrived too late to reunite with his father had been devastating; he would always live with that bitter disappointment. *But I certainly arrived in time to be a big help to Mother and the girls.* He consoled himself with that thought.

His time away from home and in the Sudbury mine had taught him how much he needed to be part of a family, and he was proud of himself for the role he had assumed. He had also come to an important realization: *I know I could never take Father's place, but that's not what anybody expects of me anyway.* Just understanding that simple fact eased much of the burden of responsibility he'd placed on himself.

Caleb enjoyed working on the Whylie farm, and he liked living in the village where there were other boys his age with whom he could spend some of his free time. Even Andrew Whylie was acting surprisingly civil toward him.

Yesterday, Caleb had heard Andrew practising his fiddle and recognized a Christmas carol. He couldn't believe his ears when Mrs. Whylie whispered that Andrew was planning a surprise for the party tonight. *What a change from that day I first arrived home! I was so hungry and shabby and scared to death after meeting up with Mr. Whylie and his gun.* Thinking of that incident now made him chuckle.

Before he knew it, he was walking up the lane to home. His heart lifted to see the warm and welcoming light of a coal oil lamp through the frost-encrusted window on this dark December afternoon.

As he greeted his family, he couldn't resist asking if anyone had seen the Ghost of Christmas Past yet, to which his sisters all said with a groan, "Oh, Ca-leb!"

"Well, you said this house was haunted," he teased.

A couple of hours after his arrival, there was a knock at the door. Caleb and his excited sisters rushed to greet their first guests.

"Merry Christmas, Caleb." Dr. Paul greeted him with a big smile and a handshake.

"Yes, merry Christmas, Caleb, and happy birthday, Briar!" his daughter called out.

Before Caleb could even say merry Christmas in return, his mother called out from behind him, "Come in. Come in. You're just in time to help with the Christmas tree. Caleb, please take our guests' cloaks and hang them up."

He couldn't help smiling at the excitement in her voice. As he stood with outstretched arms, the Pauls piled on snowy cloaks, hats, and gloves. The heavy load gave off the peculiar musty smell of damp wool.

"Sleigh bells! I hear sleigh bells!" cried Samantha. Rascal, picking up on her excitement, gave two belated barks.

While Caleb hung up the Pauls' coats and hats, Samantha scraped a thin film of frost from the front window so she could peer out. "It's them! The Whylies are here!"

Briar opened the door, and another cheerful chorus of "Welcome!" "Happy birthday!" and "Merry Christmas!" echoed in the cabin.

Looking around the room with its welcoming fire and bright paper ornaments, Caleb absorbed every detail as if to stamp them on his brain forever, especially the shining faces of his sisters, the kindly faces of his family's new friends, Miss Paul and her father, and the Whylies. Even Andrew had managed a "Merry Christmas"!

Home! Caleb almost shouted it out loud. *This is where I belong!*

***

After dinner, everyone stood around the tree they had just finished decorating, admiring their handiwork and exclaiming that this was surely the best Christmas tree ever. Andrew removed his fiddle from its bag and began playing softly.

"'Silent Night'! Oh, how lovely! It's my favourite." Heather Paul's eyes glistened.

Andrew blushed, Mrs. Whylie wiped away a tear, and Dr. Paul began to hum along with the tune. Soon a variety of voices joined him with the words; some sang high and sweet, some deep and gruff, one or two decidedly off-key, but all with hearty feeling.

Mother produced a steaming bowl of fruit punch and the birthday cake, decorated with a sprig of fresh holly. She began to propose a toast to family and good friends but, overcome with emotion, came to a sudden stop in mid-sentence.

In that moment of quiet, as everyone stood holding their punch cups, waiting for the toast to continue, an unexpected memory rose in Caleb's mind of something his father had loved to say at Christmas. Raising his own cup high, he stepped forward and quoted Tiny Tim from Dickens's *A Christmas Carol:*

"God bless us, every one!"

A Favour, Please

Would you kindly take a minute to rate this book (1-5 stars) and/or leave a comment at www.wendytruscott.com
or http://www.facebook.com/hauntedjourney/

Thank you.

Author's Notes:

I have borrowed the names of friends and family members for some characters in *Haunted Journey* to honour them, and I hope they enjoy what I've written. These characters do not in any way, however, reflect the true ages, physical descriptions, or natures of the real people. Only one horse, one dog, and one monkey remain true to their names and characters, but they are unlikely to know!

The characters Tom Big Canoe and Jonah portray the goodwill and helpfulness shown by most First Nations people towards settlers, many of whom could not have survived without their assistance. Although the word "Indian" is not in favour now, it was commonly used at the time of the story. I have included notes below about two places in the story named for prominent First Nations people.

The particular village and farms described in this story are not found on any maps. I have left their location to the individual reader's imagination, because they represent the many similar pioneer villages and farms all over Muskoka.

The farmhouse of pine logs shown on the back cover was Henry Edward and Elizabeth Hare's from Stephenson Township, 1872. The Hares lived here for thirty-two years and raised fourteen children. It is currently located, along with a collection of other fine heritage buildings, at Muskoka Heritage Place, Huntsville, Ontario, and represents perfectly, the Lawson family's cabin in this story, complete with the stump where the children's mother liked to sit with a cup of tea.

www.muskokaheritageplace.org   (photo credit: the author)

<u>Muskoka:</u> Chief Musqua Ukie or Musqua Ukee, also known as Chief William Yellowhead, born about 1769, served with the British during the War of 1812. Named chief of the Deer tribe of the Chippewa (Ojibwa) Indians in 1816, he settled with his band at the site of Orillia in 1830 in accordance with lieutenant-Governor Colborne's plan for gathering nomadic tribes on reserves. Pressure from white settlers forced the Indians to relinquish their land and Yellowhead's band moved to Rama in 1838-1839. It is believed that the Muskoka District, which embraced his hunting grounds, was named after this greatly respected chief who died in 1864 and was buried in St. James' churchyard, Orillia.

<u>Bigwin Island</u> on Lake of Bays is named for Ojibwa Chief Joseph Bigwin (or Big Wind). Families based at places like Rama and Beausoleil Island travelled to the Muskoka region in spring to establish gardens as well as to hunt and trade in the area around their settlements. Joseph Bigwin, from Rama, who distinguished himself in the War of 1812, had his settlement on Bigwin Island in Lake of Bays and at Cedar Narrows, now Dorset. The original developers of Bigwin Inn consented to preserve and protect the multiple ancient <u>native</u> burial grounds on the island from desecration and to allow Chief John Bigwin, who was still alive at the time, to be buried there with his ancestors when he died.

Acknowledgments and Appreciation

To the late Melody Richardson, Writer-in-Residence at the Baysville and Bracebridge Libraries, for her constant encouragement and constructive criticism. Melody saw the beginning of a novel in one of my essays and convinced me I could write this story.

To the members of the Baysville and Bracebridge Libraries Writers' Circles and the Muskoka Authors' Association for their encouragement and practical help. At the risk of forgetting someone, I want to thank the following people especially: Wendie Donabie and Cindy Watson, dedicated founders of the M.A.A., for providing a forum for writers to improve and share their craft; Jacqueline Opresnik (Package from the Past);Sharyn Heagle (A Clear Range of Vision); Yvonne Heath (Love Your Life to Death); Geordie Heath; Judy Snodden (Finding Joy, a Mother's Journey through Grief); Sherry Rondeau (Dear Tony, a Caregiver's Journal); Denise Marcelli(Journey to Survival); and David Franks ('D'-Tales); for their helpful advice on the process of publishing. To the readers of my early drafts, Caleb and Chantal Truscott, Jean and Don Murray, and Dr. Sheila Pennington, for their patience and helpful suggestions. To Ruby and Violet Gray, and their mother, Cindy McGlynn, who read this story to them at bedtime, for their enthusiasm.

To Tara Truscott and Stephen Drury for their attention to detail in proofreading the final draft.

To Paul Truscott, Jr. for his great patience in answering cries for help with formatting.

To Lizann Flatt (Flattout Books) for her kindness in being a mentor and for her excellent guidance on my early drafts.

To Caroline Kaiser, editor, www.carolinekaiser.com, whose expertise saved me from many errors and improved my efforts immensely. Any remaining mistakes are mine alone.

To Stan Mackinnon and the late Jack Hammond III for answering my questions about their families' pioneer experiences.

To the staff at the Baysville Library and the Baysville Friends of the Library for their priceless contributions to their community.

Above all, to my husband, Paul, for his constant love and belief in me, and to my family for their love and the joy they bring me. You truly are the sunshine in my life.